Casca awoke, the effects of the opiate having worn off. The darkness of the coffin enveloped him. The same desperate fear he had felt as a slave in the mines of Greece returned. To be buried alive, unable to die. *How long would the darkness last . . . one year . . . five . . . for eternity?*

He beat his head against the silken pillows. "*Alive, the bitch has buried me alive. How can I find the Jew if I am buried here?*"

Casca was still, his body unmoving. Once every twenty minutes his pulse beat and every forty minutes his chest would move slowly. His system came to an almost complete halt. Like the great bears of the ice mountains, Casca slept.

The years passed. . .

Charter Books by Barry Sadler

CASCA #1: THE ETERNAL MERCENARY
CASCA #2: GOD OF DEATH
CASCA #3: THE WAR LORD
CASCA #4: PANZER SOLDIER
CASCA #5: THE BARBARIAN
CASCA #6: THE PERSIAN
CASCA #7: THE DAMNED
CASCA #8: SOLDIER OF FORTUNE
CASCA #9: THE SENTINEL

THE WAR LORD

#3

BARRY SADLER

CHARTER BOOKS, NEW YORK

CASCA: THE WAR LORD

A Charter Book / published by arrangement with the author

PRINTING HISTORY
First Charter edition / April 1980
Seventh printing / September 1983

ISBN: 0-441-09221-7

Charter Books are published by The Berkley Publishing Group, 200 Madison Avenue, New York, N.Y. 10016.
PRINTED IN THE UNITED STATES OF AMERICA

CASCA:
THE WAR LORD

One

The dank Boston fog wrapped itself around the stocky figure standing in the shadows, just barely visible from the firefly-glow of the street light on the corner. Even in the dark, the street had that aura of old money and wealth.

The man stood there, his broad shoulders stooped as if he were older than he looked; like some contemporary Atlas, he seemed to carry the weight of the world on his shoulders. He raised his eyes and looked down the street to the two-story brick house that had held his attention for the last two hours. Straightening suddenly, he shook his head and shoulders as if throwing off a fleeting chill, or perhaps making up his mind.

Stepping from the shadows, he made his way across the street to the steps leading to his objective. In the dull glow of the street lamp, he read the large brass plaque beside the door: JULIUS GOLDMAN, M.D. The light reflecting from the brass plaque shone on the hairline scar which ran from the man's left eye to the corner of his mouth, creating a slightly sardonic grin which never left him, except in a rage. A fleeting gold shadow was thrown across his eyes as he raised his hand to the brass knocker in the shape of a lion's head. The Lion of Judah?

The sudden sharp rapping of the door knocker broke through the damp silence of the night. He waited and then knocked again. The door opened, revealing a severely dressed, middle-aged woman, her hair in a tight bun. She had the air of authority of a trusted and efficient housekeeper.

"Yes?" Her voice had the same severity as her looks with just a touch of snobbishness. "What is it?" She looked him up and down with that slight moué of distaste maitre d's often display when someone does not appear worthy of their attention. "Speak up, man." Then, not giving the man at the door a chance to answer: "The doctor sees no patients at home unless it's an emergency."

The man raised his eyes to the woman and locked them; the light grey-blue color of his eyes seemed even paler in the half-light of the open doorway. When he spoke, his voice was deep and masculine.

"Woman, shut up."

The housekeeper began to retort indignantly that no one ever spoke to her in that manner. Then she saw the look of steel behind the man's eyes and ice water raced through her bowels. Her voice changed, taking on tones of submission and fear.

"I-I'm sorry, but the doctor has company tonight. Is he expecting you?" she carefully avoided looking into the intruder's eyes.

The stranger extended his hand to her, fist

closed. As she looked at the back of the scarred knuckles and wrist, he said quietly, wearily, his voice almost a sigh, "Take this to your master. I believe he will wish to see me."

He stepped inside against her silent protest, the deep strength of the figure transmitted through his bearing told her here was a man not to take liberties with. She took the small tobacco sack he extended and started to look inside.

"Don't," came the instant sharp response from the visitor. Again she had the icy feel of fear. Involuntarily she bowed her head.

"Yes, sir," she whispered and scurried away.

From the dining room the sound of laughter drifted back to the man along with the smell of rich food and good cigars. The housekeeper did her duty, handing the sack to her master and then rapidly excusing herself for the rest of the evening on the pretext she was feeling ill and would be in her room until morning.

Julius Goldman opened the sack. A small shining object fell into his palm, gleaming almost like gold. His heart skipped a beat as he looked at the bronze arrowhead. Sweat appeared instantly on his brow and upper lip. Standing so rapidly he almost knocked over his chair, he addressed his guests: "Gentlemen, I am sorry, but I have an emergency to attend to. Enjoy the food and wine; leave when you please as I don't know when I will be returning, this might take some time. Now if you will excuse me. . ."

He turned, not waiting for any questions and made his way to the foyer where his strange guest waited. The sight of the square back and muscled neck brought the smell of blood back to him—blood from the hospital in Vietnam where he had taken the arrowhead from the leg of the man.

"Casey? Casey, is it you?"

The man turned. Slowly and wearily he reached out and took the arrowhead from the doctor's hand put it into his own coat pocket. He smiled a crooked, almost shy grin.

"Good evening, Doctor, it has been a while. When we last met, I meant to leave the arrowhead with you, but thought it would be a good calling card if ever I needed to see you again. It seems there is a compulsion for me to finish what was started that night in the Eighth Field Hospital in Nam and again at the Museum. Do you wish to continue?"

Gulping, Goldman nodded in the affirmative, indicating the way to his study with a sweep of his hand. The man called Casey took his wet coat off and hung it carefully on the hall tree by the door.

He walked into the study scanning the well-stocked bookshelves, noting titles and authors. Touching a leather-bound copy of Machiavelli's, *The Prince*, he commented: "Surprising reading for a surgeon, Doctor Goldman. It's odd how this little book has survived and influenced so many people since he wrote it. I told him not to publish it, but he always did want things his way, though out of friendship he kept it in his desk for five years. After he died, however, he did have his way and it was printed. I believe you would have liked him as I did. He was quite bright, if somewhat of an opportunist and agitator."

Goldman stuttered, then, clearing his throat,

"You knew him? You knew Machiavelli?"

Casey chuckled deeply, "Yes, good Doctor. It appears we need to refresh your memory. Here, sit down and be comfortable."

The irresistable quality of Casey's voice froze Goldman to his seat, unaware that he had obeyed Casey's command. Casey faced him, his grey-blue eyes seeming to fill the room.

"Yes, Doctor, I knew Machiavelli and many others. Remember me, who I am, what I am and where I am from? That's right, Doctor, come with me, back again to where our story left off. Remember Jesus and the Crucifixion?"

Goldman was aware of nothing other than the compelling voice and eyes of Casey as they drew him out of his present reality and threw him back into another plane of being, one in which the man called Casey had stood at the foot of the cross of Jesus and driven his spear into the side of Christ.

The crucifixion scenario flashed again before him, the storm and wind, the darkness; the terrible face of Jesus as he looked down upon the Roman soldier who had just driven a spear into his side, a Roman soldier named Casca Aufio Longinus, born in the reign of the Great Julius.

The Jew's words struck at his mind again as he heard Casca repeat the statement that led to his fate. When the spear was withdrawn, blood poured from the side of Jesus and the Messiah looked down upon the Roman, his voice great with an unknown power, his eyes blazing: "Soldier, you are content with what you are, then that you shall remain until we meet again. As I go now to my Father, you must one day come to me . . . Soldier, you are content with what you are . . . then that you shall remain until we meet again."

He again saw Casca wipe a bloody hand across his mouth where the blood of Jesus touched his tongue, then fell into a spasm of burning anguish while his body was purified; the legionary lay whimpering like a hurt animal with the voice of Jesus echoing in his mind. "*Until we meet again.*"

Like a speeding movie camera, Casca's voice led him through a rapid repeat of his history; slavery in the mines of Greece; the Roman arena where the tricks taught him by the Chinese sage led to his freedom and again to slavery in the Imperial War galleys; Parthia, where outside the walls of doomed Ctesiphon, a bronze arrowhead had lodged in his leg; Viking longships raced over the oceans to the land of the Teotec and Olmecs; the Pyramids; a mask of jade and daggers of flint and obsidian; cutting the beating hearts out of victims to be sacrificed to the gods.

Casca's voice drew him down again with the feeling of being in a plane, flying low over the earth until the greater reality of Casca's existence wiped out his own.

He was there.

Waves as tall as mountains were raging and whipping the red-striped sails of the dragon-prowed longships into shreds, driving them on.

Two

The waves rushed over him filling his mouth with brine, trying to force air from his lungs, plunging him down into the dark and then raising him again, his grip locked in the lines of the broken piece of mast to which he clung.

His stomach and lungs emptied themselves repeatedly, spewing out salt water and bile. White storms of froth whipped up by the raging winds lashed his face and eyes until they were almost swollen shut.

The two Viking longships were long since out of sight, the storm pushing them on: To what? Home or death? Their crews tried frantically to keep their ships from being dragged under the waves as the dragon-headed prows plunged into each succeeding watery mountain and rose again to face the next series of rising and falling mountains and valleys.

Casca groaned as the rope lines wrapped around his arms threatened to pull them from the sockets. Opening his mouth to catch a quick breath, he was dragged under again and again. The night seemed endless; but, as things must, it too came to an end when, with the grey light of the false dawn, the storm passed. The waters calmed into long rising swells and hollows and almost as quickly as the winds came they left.

With the easing of the storm, Casca pulled himself lengthwise onto the broken mast, legs and arms dangling in the water, unmindful of the daring, darting little fish that surfaced to take timid nibbles at toes and fingers and dart away to safety.

He slept.

By midday the sun had burned away the last remnants of the storm, the waves were now gentle steady swells, following the tides. A familiar sound broke through to Casca's subconscious, drawing him out of the dark of his mind back into reality. The sound kept pounding at him until he opened his salt-encrusted eyes, red-rimmed and sore. The sound of oars slapping the water in unison came to him, now punctuated by the distant cursing of the oarsmaster. From its apparent lack of a ramming beam on the prow, Casca assumed it was a trading ship. As it neared, Casca tried to yell, though to no avail as his throat was too swollen to get any appreciable amount of noise out. The sound issuing from his cracked and swollen lips resembled more of a squeak than a yell.

It didn't matter. The oarsmen were shipping their tools and laying them on the sides, already regretting the future fact of the amount of labor it would take to get the ship under way again after stopping. The vessel's master, a tough-looking, barrel-chested, bowlegged Sicilian from Syracuse, had spotted Casca in the water and ordered the oars to stop their incessant slapping.

A line was tossed to him as the merchant ship wallowed in the swells. After several attempts, the ship and mast piece got their timing together and Casca freed himself from the safety line he had used through the night and grabbed the line from the ship. The wet hawser slipped between his hands, taking off chunks of skin from his swollen fingers, but a knot in the line was held as it tried to pass through, jerking him from the mast, back into the waves and then up again. Casca spit water while the captain and crew looked on laughed.

"Listen, you water dog, if you want out of the drink, you better hold on. I can't hang around here all day waiting for you to get on board. The Saxons have been raiding these waters for the last two years, so either climb that line and get your ass on board, or I'll cut you loose and you can make it to Britannia on your own; it's only twelve leagues to the port."

The thought of spending another night in the drink gave Casca the impetus needed to drag himself to the side of the ship where waiting hands hauled him on board. "None too gently," he thought. The captain laughed as the men tossed Casca on the deck minus a goodly portion of skin. His laughter stilled when he saw the short sword and scars.

"Well man, are you a citizen?" Then clearing his throat: "You're carrying a soldier's blade, so I presume you have done some. Who are you and how did you end up here?"

Casca paused, giving himself time to think. Did he say the Saxons were raiding? Pulling himself erect, he faced the ship's master.

"Yes, sir, to both questions, and as to how I got here, it's simple enough. I was hired on as guard on a grain ship out of Messillia when a Saxon raider overtook us and we had to go off course to get away; then the storm hit and I don't know where the Hades we are, or if the ship went down or survived. I was washed overboard and spent the night hanging to the damned mast."

The captain nodded. The story made sense. Still, it was too bad the man was freeborn, he would have brought a good price in the slave markets.

Lucanus Ortius put his hands on his hips as he addressed his new guest: "Well, you're in luck. We are only two days from the port of Dubrae. I'll put you ashore there. There's always plenty of work in Britannia for one who knows the way of the sword. And from the looks of those cuts on your hide, you have had plenty of intimacy with one, though that large one on your chest looks as if it should have done you in. But, no matter, you are welcome to my hospitality for the next two days. Find yourself a niche in the crew's section. They will have some dry clothes for you and a hammock. Then come and see me after you have fed and rested. Now, I have to get back to running this overaged scow and get her under way."

Signalling the Hortator, the man began to beat on the skin drumhead. "Prepare to row, set your oars." The mixed complement of freedmen and slaves did as they were ordered with an understandable amount of grumbling.

Casca felt a twinge as they set the oar blades into the sea and began to pull in time with the beat of the drum. How long ago had it been when he slaved under the oarsmaster's lash on the war galleys of Rome?

Casca fed on pickled pork and thin wine and hit the sack, sleeping until the first light of the next day. Upon arising he felt refreshed. The Latin chatter of the ship's crew brought memories and left him feeling somewhat nostalgic. The crew was friendly enough though distant; the stranger had an aura to him that said move carefully around him and don't come up on his back unexpected.

Climbing out of the hatch, Casca went to the side of the single-banked ship and emptied his bladder into the coastal waters of Britannia. Land was already in sight through the low bank of clouds and fog that was hugging the water by the coastline. The wind was with them now and the bow was slicing clean through the waves. With a sense of smugness, he compared the wallowing trader of Rome with his own sleek ships and found the Roman version a poor second.

Already thoughts and memories of the last years were fading into the recesses of his mind. "Change, always change, but still the same . . . just different faces."

Making his way along the deck to where Lucanus Ortius stood by the tiller, he ran his eyes over the vessel. The condition of a ship and attitude of a crew and slaves could tell a man a lot about the master. Clean, neat ropes curled, no garbage on this deck. The crew looked healthy and that they did a little bitching—even the slaves—said this was a good ship. The master demanded performance, but appeared well-liked.

Spying Casca, the captain motioned for him to join him on the upper deck where the dark sailor from the Aegean guided the ship through the rocky coastal waters.

Ortius stood, a wine cup in his hand, the wind

from behind whipping his leg wrappings, a turban of red linen protecting his balding pate from the elements.

"Welcome aboard the Naida. I can see you got your sea legs and from the way your hide's been burned by the sun, you have spent a long time in the eastern regions of the empire, right?"

"Aye, Captain. I was on a trader out of Pireaus for the last few years and this trip was the first for me to these waters."

The captain nodded, pleased his deduction was correct, "Your name, man?"

Casca caught his balance as the ship crested some white water, "Longinus, Casca Longinus."

Lucanus Ortius prided himself on being a judge of men. "From the looks of you, Master Longinus, I would say you have been around a bit; those cut marks on your hide look to be enough for five or six men to have died from."

Sea spray whipped over the deck, freshening Casca's face. "Aye, Captain, I have been carved up a bit, but they are not as bad as they look. Dull blades don't cut deep, just gouge out a lot of meat, and I still have some to spare."

Ortius liked the look of the man before him, a strong looking rascal and one you could not easily scare.

"Good enough. As a courtesy to a castaway, you will be my guest. Just don't start any trouble and we'll make port tomorrow. We lost some way in the night and the damned winds have shifted again; my oarsmen could barely keep their own against it and we couldn't set sails until just before dawn. Now, I have duties to attend to, make yourself comfortable and perhaps we'll talk later. I used to have some shipmates who worked out of Pireaus, perhaps you'll know them." The bandy-legged barrel-chested little Sicilian laughed at the memory. "Remind me to tell you about the whorehouse in the south of the village where a Greek whore tried to castrate me for short changing her."

Casca laughed; the scar running from his left eye to his cheek seemed to tingle.

The day turned bright and clear as they tacked first to port and starboard working against the cross angles of the wind as the sea miles dropped steadily behind. Casca spent the rest of the day cleaning his weapons, wiping the salt from his blade and honing down the edge of his double-edged dagger he kept in his leggings. During his years in the north countries, he had grown used to having them on and continued to wear them.

He looked out seaward back across the distance he had come on the Viking longship, wending its way to the safety of the Keep at Helsfjord. "Another part of my life gone . . . Wassail, Olaf Glamson, take my ships home, and if your father lives, tell him I still walk this earth—though I believe he would know it anyway, that great ugly bear of a man. The wheel of life turned again."

In the flickering waters, for a moment, he saw the face of Liu Shao Tze, the sage from the lands of far Khitai, who had taught him the way of open-hand fighting. Automatically, he turned his head to face the East. "Khitai, perhaps it's time for me to see the lands beyond the Indus."

"Sail off the starboard," the lookouts cried.

Instantly, every head turned to see what vessel was approaching. Unable to make her out, the captain cried up to the lookout perched on top of the single mast, "Can you make her out?"

"Aye, Captain. I will wager my bonus she's a Saxon; the cut of her sails tell me that and the wind is with her. She'll be on us in less than an hour."

The captain spit, "Saxons, damn them all to the bowels of the darkest pit in hades. One more day and we would have made port. Keep your eye on her and tell me if she changes her course. All hands on deck, prepare for boarders!"

The crew rushed to the weapons rack taking out their personal preferences from pikes to axes. Several had bows but not enough; with enough archers, they probably would be able to keep the raider at a distance until nightfall and lose them in the fogs that always came to the coast of this land when the dark settled.

"A good crew, no panic," thought Casca as he watched the look of grim determination set in on the faces of the crew and slaves alike.

The slaves too took up weapons, Ortius having made all his slaves a bargain: "Serve me for three years and you will be given your letter of manumission." This bargain had been to his benefit in the past and was one of the reasons that he had so little trouble from his slaves' part, they knew the captain would keep his word and it would still be better to be an oar slave than to be taken by those long-haired bearded devils called Saxons. It was said they ate the hearts of their prisoners and sacrificed them to their terrible gods.

Casca moved to the side of the captain. "Sir, have you ever fought the Saxons before?"

Ortius looked Casca in the face and saw a change that sent a shiver over him. "No, but I have talked to those that have and they are wild animals. This day we win, or die."

Casca grunted, fingering his sword hilt. "I've fought them several times. They are poor archers, but when it comes to close quarters, they are the best axe men on the face of the earth. Most carry two or more throwing axes which they can throw in unison to keep their enemies undercover for a moment while they rush and throw themselves like a pack of dogs onto their opponents, using a combination of axes and lances. The bastards are tough, Captain. But I have beaten them before and have no intention of losing this time either."

The Saxon ship was in sight now, closing fast. The faces of her wild crew became rapidly discernable, wild men with long flowing hair blowing to the front from the wind behind, their mustaches and beards giving them an even wilder look under the horned helmets and conical steel caps. Across the water, battle cries could be heard as they worked themselves into a killer frenzy.

Ortius ordered the cooking fire extinguished and all hands to stand by to repel boarders. The fat trader was no match for the swift raider. But Ortius was no coward and donned a breastplate of antique armor he had picked up in Bithynia. Casca recalled when it had been the newest style among the wealthy young nobles of the Eques, the Cavalry.

Casca placed himself, watching carefully for the spot where the two vessels would join and the raiders would toss their grappling hooks to tie them together in an umbilical cord of death.

As they neared the raider, Casca thought one wild looking bastard looked vaguely familiar but underneath all that hair it was difficult to tell. As the Romans said, "All barbarians look alike."

All thoughts of the past months fled. The basic soldier in Casca came to the fore. As his pulse rate increased, he took short sharp breaths, pumping oxygen into his system automatically. He began to call out orders, commanding the sailors nearest the side to get ready and duck on his order.

Ortius looked at him and, seeing a man who knew his business, said nothing, just nodding in agreement for the others to follow Casca's lead. The captain knew ships, but this was different. In Casca, he recognized a professional and in this instant he made the decision to turn the order of the battle over to this stranger from the sea.

"Do as the soldier orders," he bellowed, loud enough for the Saxons less than a hundred yards away to hear.

The sailors huddled together instinctively, and Casca roared at them to separate to make smaller targets for the wave of axes that would come.

The Saxon ship began to close alongside the trader. Their leader stood in the bow, a massively built man with blond-grey flowing hair and mustache, axe held high. With his downward stroke, the Saxons rose to throw. Casca waiting for this moment, cried out to the sailors to fall flat on their faces; the sheer force of his order made most of them hit the deck like they had been pole-axed. Those too late to obey, had their skulls and chests laid open by the wave of thrown axes that raced across the small distance separating the two ships. As the axes were thrown, so were the grappling hooks and before the death cry of the stricken sailors could really begin, the Saxons were hauling the two ships side by side, the wood giving a strange muffled shriek as they dragged together. The Saxons crowded at the side, standing on the railing, ready to leap aboard the trader.

In their eagerness, two fell into the water between the ships and were mashed into a protoplasmic red jelly when the waves brought them back together again, leaving only a red stain on each ship to show that here had been two men who were no more.

"Up and at them!" The command stirred the defenders and they rose in time to catch the Saxons at their most vulnerable point when they were attempting the crossing from their ship to the trader. Normally the barrage of thrown axes would have given them the necessary seconds to make an uncontested assault, but now they faced desperate men with pikes in their hands and murder in their hearts.

The Saxons were stopped. But only for a moment. Then the leader of the enemy ship threw himself across the gap, landing on board. He began striking down sailors left and right, caving in skulls and chests, as he cleared an area through which the rest of his band eagerly followed.

The seamen were no match in close combat for the ferocity of the German pirates and were easily being forced back. More and more Saxons rushed into the bridgehead created by their leader, Skoldbjorn, who was slicing down all who opposed him, bellowing for Thor to give him strength to kill all who dared to stand in front of his axe, which was red and dripping with the lifeblood of the sailors. His whirling attack came to a sudden stop as his axe was knocked back with enough force that it left his arm and hand tingling.

Casca pushed him back using a combination of

sword and dagger; thrust, jab, strike high, then low. Casca dodged a blow to the head that would have split him to the chest and whirled low to the deck pivoting in a tight circle, slicing the hamstring muscles of a Saxon who came close. Then, raising himself under the guard of the leader, they locked, the Saxon's axe barring Casca's Gladius Iberius, while his other hand held the dagger away from his stomach where it was only millimeters away from opening him up like a gutted fish.

They broke away and locked again, two strong men face to face; again they broke, then whirled around each other like madmen, striking, parrying, sparks leaping when their blades met. The force of their combat brought the rest of the fighting to a stand-still. The protagonists from the two ships separated, keeping a wary eye on each other while the two in the center of the deck met again and again like charging bulls. They grappled, faces touching.

The Saxon spoke between clenched teeth, "Who are you? I have seen you before."

They broke again and Casca made a deep lunging attack that changed in midstroke to a swipe to the gut, leaving a thin line of red across the Saxon's muscled belly.

"I am the man who is going to kill you, barbarian. I am Casca, the Roman."

The Saxon stumbled back, nearly falling over a pile of ropes. "Casca from Helsfjord, the Walker?" Terror slipped into his voice and for the first time courage began to slip away from him. "You're dead. You sailed to the ends of the earth."

Casca struck a blow that numbed his own arm to the shoulder and knocked the horned helmet off the Saxon's head.

"I'm back."

The Saxon countered, forcing Casca back. They separated, each gasping trying to catch his breath.

"You must be over sixty. My father, Hegsten, fought you at the field of Runes over thirty years ago."

Remembrance flashed. "Yes, Saxon dog and whore, I only chopped the left arm off the sire, I am going to kill the pup."

Casca sliced down in a long stroke that forced the axe up high to counter; as the steel from the blade and the axe met, Casca gave a strange sliding movement obliquely that turned his opponent half around unable to use his free hand. Then Casca's dagger slid to the hilt between the striated muscles of the abdomen, sinking deep within, the point of the blade puncturing the great artery running along the spine, letting the Saxon's lifeblood flow into his abdominal cavity.

Pulling the Saxon to him and holding his opponent like a lover, Casca plunged the blade deeper into him, moving the hilt from side to side, severing organs. The death glaze was already creeping over the Saxon's eyes, fogging them.

Through blood-flecked lips he whispered, "You are he. The Walker."

He died shuddering, his last act to raise his head back, throat cords standing out from the strain, then drew his last breath. "*Odin.*" The name of his god echoed across the water.

Casca raised his body, grunting with the strain and tossed the carcass over the side. The raiders were still, silent, shocked. Their leader had fallen.

Sensing this was the moment, Casca cried out to the crew, "Kill! Kill!" He rushed the stunned barbarians like a whirlwind, his blade and dagger doing bloody work. The crew hesitated but a moment and then followed cheering.

The Saxons broke. Their leader dead, their courage left them. They fled back to their ship across lines, leaping the span separating the two ships. Several fell into the waters, but none gave them aid.

The trader crew cut the lines of the grappling hooks mooring them together and the ships parted, Ortius' crew cheering.

The Saxons backed water to get away from what they had thought to be easy pickings, instead proving to be a shark; several of which were already tugging at the bodies in the water, taking the living along with the dead.

Ortius quickly resumed command. "Back to your post and oars, you miserable sea lice. Clear the Saxon scum from my decks and send them to their brothers to feed the hungry ones below."

The battle was over.

Casca, as usual, after a fight, felt drained, his limbs trembling, not only from physical exhaustion, but from the emotional release as well. Breathing deeply, he gulped down air. "It is over."

Ortius slapped him on the back. "By Poseidon's green sea beard! It was a lucky day when we found you bobbing like a cork. You have made a friend this day, Casca Longinus, and never let it be said that Ortius, the ship's master, forgets a debt. When we make port I am going to buy the ten best whores in town and see if they can kill you. By Jupiter's brass balls man, I never saw such fight in all my life!"

Three
DUBRAE

No further incidents interrupted the journey of the trader to the safe port of Dubrae from which on a clear day the coast of Gaul could almost be seen across the channel. The crew was in good spirits; their valor increased with each retelling of the battle and had multiplied several fold by the time the city came into view as a light colored speck on the hills behind.

There were enough souvenirs left behind by the Saxons so that everyone on board had a trophy to attest to his courage: helmets with horns, swords, and enough of those terrible throwing axes so that even each slave had at least one.

Ortius, pleased at the way the oarslaves had fought alongside his freedmen, knocked a year off his deal with them and several were to be given their letters of manumission as soon as a magistrate could be found to witness and document the releases.

The trader slipped into port under a fair wind, passing several others on their way out, carrying cargos of tin and wool to the Empire and beyond. Like all ports, this one had its own particular blend of the odors of fish and garbage. The town itself was set upon a small group of hills that faced the channel. The immediate area around the port was lined with docks and piers along with a tannery and several warehouses, adding their scents to the already pungent atmosphere.

In this area also were the places for sailors and their like: wine ships and inns along with an undetermined number of whorehouses catering—for the right price—to all tastes. The homes and businesses near the hillsides were for the upper classes. Several villas had obviously been built in the Roman style; here the captains of the ships found amusement.

Ortius gave his men their unloading orders, then, accompanied by Casca, left to present his papers to the port authority. There he declared his cargo and paid his duty, accidentally dropping a purse of silver denarii as they left, to insure the amount and kind of cargo he declared were not too closely looked at by the customs officials.

Taking Casca by the arm, he guided him through the labyrinth of streets and alleys, past shops and vendors, eating stalls and racks of drying fish.

"Well, my overmuscled friend, before we do anything else, we have to get you into some decent clothes; these rags you are wearing would embarrass a Dacian goatherder, though you have the smell to go with the description."

Stopping at a shuttered door, he pounded upon it for admittance. "Open up, you hooked robber of decent seafaring men, let us in to see the rags you try to pass off as clothes!" Ortius kicked away a short-haired dog which sniffed tentatively and then raised its leg over Ortius' shin. Yelping, it raced down the street before completing an act of defilement.

After hours of haggling, Ortius grumbling and clucking over prices, Casca's clothes finally met his friend's approval: a short tunic of plain blue wool spun locally and a cloak of burgandy from Gaul, along with a broad belt of Spanish leather, set with large brass studs. A new set of caligulae, Roman style military boots that laced up to the calves, finished his wardrobe. Adjusting the strap of his halberd, so that his sword hung properly, Casca looked at the effect in a polished bronze mirror and was not displeased by what he saw.

"By Mirtha, I'm still a pretty good looking rascal."

Three other tunics would be delivered later to the combination inn and whorehouse Ortius had selected as their domicile while in Dubrae.

Leading the Roman along through the streets like a ship hauling a dingy behind it, the bandy-legged Sicilian kept up a rambling discourse on the faults and merits of ladies of pleasure at the Inn of Paetius the Greek.

Laughing, they reached the entrance of the two-storied structure. Nudging Casca in the ribs, Ortius whispered, "Watch out for Paetius, he's the most notorious faggot in the country, but for all that is a good fellow who has clean rooms and doesn't water the wine to excess; he charges only slightly more than his wares are worth, but most important—he has the cleanest girls in town. So you won't have to worry about leaving here with a touch of the pox."

Bursting into the smoky interior, the barrel-chested sailor pushed his way through the crowd bellowing, "Wine for my man. We have been raping and ravaging since dawn . . . wine do you hear . . . when we had some spare time we killed a hundred Saxons . . . *wine!* Ortius the great is here, accompanied by one almost as handsome and brave!"

The crowd roared with laughter. Obviously Ortius was well known and liked. A massive figure swept down upon them; Casca prepared himself for a fight. The huge man reached Ortius first, swept him up into his arms raising him a foot off the wooden floor, kissing the struggling Sicilian on both cheeks as fat tears ran down the cheeks of Paetius the Greek.

Paetius was six-foot-six and close to three hundred pounds, most of it muscle. His finely sculptured face had an aquiline nose which seemed too small sitting on top of the mass of meat. Several knife scars were visible on his neck and arms, attesting to the fact that here was one hell of a pansy.

Squirming out of the giant's grasp, Ortius checked his rib cage and then introduced Casca to the Greek, who immediately performed an identical assault on Casca much to his chagrin, but as the man was obviously so good natured, it was hard to take offense, at least until Paetius pinched him on the ass. But the Greek set him free before Casca could respond.

Paetius lisped in a girlish voice, "Ortius, I have been so worried about you, those horrible barbarians have been attacking almost everything that floats; it's been terrible for business. But, enough of my troubles," he said, wiping a tear of joy from his eye, "at least now I know another of my chicks has come home safely."

Calling to his tavern wenches, he threw three sailors from their seats to make room for Ortius and Casca. Ignoring their complaints, he silenced them with a stern upheld forefinger and they meekly acquiesced.

"Wine, you sluts, and the good stuff, none of the local vinegar."

The three settled into benches by the fireplace over which a spit of lamb was roasting, the rich smell of cooking fat brought instant growlings to their stomachs. Wine was poured. The Greek was silent, giving them time to swallow half a cup and relax a bit.

"Now, my darlings, what's all this about fighting Saxons. I must hear everything you can tell about those beasts. They are terrible, though the blond hair most of them have is quite attractive. I've thought about going blond myself," he touched his oiled and curled locks with a delicate pat. "Now Ortius dear, tell me everything, especially about this new friend of yours," he minced. "I can just tell he's a delicious brute." The Greek gave a long suggestive wink at Casca.

Casca blushed self-consciously and then laughed, choking on a gulp of wine that went down the wrong pipe, leaving him sputtering and gasping, trying to catch his breath through watering eyes.

Ortius gave him a slap on the back which didn't do Casca much good, but seemed to please the Sicilian who went on, oblivious to Casca's discomfort, and related the story of the Saxon attack to Paetius. The Greek oohed and ahed at the account of Casca's slaying of the raider chieftain, fairly squirming in delighted excitement. "I just knew you were a devil when I first saw you," he said and smiled, filling Casca's cup again.

Dismissing the tale of his prowess with a wave of his hand, Casca turned his attention to the firm and well rounded mounds of female flesh that bumped his arm. "Nice. . .very nice. I always did have a fanny fetish."

Paetius noticed his interest in the girl, sighed deeply as if wounded, then shrugged, as if to say, it's your loss if that's what you like.

Ortius also noticed Casca's wandering eye checking out the tavern wenches. Leaning close to Paetius he whispered in his ear. The Greek giggled delightedly, rose, and weaved his way with tiny steps through the benches and tables out of sight.

Casca watched his departure and the leer on the queer's face. "What the hades is he up to?"

Ortius smiled and replied, "I am just being a man of my word and living up to a promise I made some time back." Saying no more on the matter, they sat back to relax and find their land legs; it still seemed as if the table were swaying slightly. The wine flowed freely and for the first time in more years than he could remember, the Roman tasted again the sweet Falernian, whose grapes grew in the sunny hills of his first home. The wine fumes settled into his brain and the world took on a rosy glow.

Ortius seemed to have an unlimited capacity for the grape and, as the evening wore on, became merely more talkative and cheerful.

After dark settled and the lamps were lit, their oily tendrils mingling with wide columns of smoke from the fireplace, twice men came to try to talk business with Ortius, but were told that it would have to wait until the morrow . . . this night there were other matters that needed attending to.

The tavern was filled to overflowing with a mixture of humanity: everything from blue-eyed northern Gauls to a couple of Picts who sat in the corner drinking their sour beer, faces painted a fading blue; a dozen tongues spoken and understood, but all had one thing in common—the seas they sailed. To them anyone who lived by choice on land was less than a man.

After an endless number of wine bowls and cups had been emptied, jugs and pots filled and refilled, they had sampled everything even remotely resembling being intoxicating that the inn had to offer. The last bout of drinking the local, homemade beer left a green taste in his mouth and Casca finally pleaded for mercy.

Ortius, pleased at his victory, gave one magnificant fart that Casca swore had a green yeasty tinge to it and said through thick slurred words, "Good enough my friend, now that you have surrendered, your room is ready, though in this place I'm not sure just how much sleep you will get. But never mind, just remember old Ortius is a man of his word, Roman." With this Ortius fell over into a pot of wine gurgling happily.

Casca followed the brown-haired little tavern

wench who led him to the rickety stairs to his room. The stairs seemed to be weaving as if he were still on the deck of the ship. The girl giggled constantly. Leaving Casca at the doorway, she fled laughing back to the bottom of the stairs and stopped, waiting.

Casca looked down at her thinking, "What the crap is wrong with that dippy little slut?"

Suddenly he was tripped and thrown to the floor as the door slammed behind him. A feminine laugh, along with a tongue pushing its way into his mouth stopped his automatic counterattack, especially when a soft hand slid under his tunic. An oil lamp was lit in the corner.

Casca froze in shock, Ortius was indeed a man of his word. Ten women from ten countries lay in wait for him, all stark naked and smiling, blondes, redheads and hot-eyed dusky maids from Syria and Egypt.

A brunette with white even teeth and laughter in her eyes stuck a rosy nippled tit in his face and cried out merrily, "Roman, I am going to screw your brains out before you get out of here."

Several of the other girls countered with, "Not if we get him first", and the melée was on! Twenty hands grabbed him, throwing him onto the three beds which had been pushed together in anticipation of the event about to take place.

In less time than it takes to flip a denaril, he was as naked as they. The girls yelped in joy. Here was a man.

Instantly he was covered in warm naked bodies, perfumed hair and thighs mingled with pressing breasts and mouths until he felt as if he were drowning in a sea of women. They piled on him, each anxious to get her fair share of the man beneath them. Lips and legs covered him from head to toe and one bitch, the Egyptian, had his big toe in her mouth sucking away. Casca squirmed in pleasure, he had never felt anything like it. The Egyptian, obviously aware of the erotic effect she was having on the scarred Roman, was content to do her part in the night's orgy.

Paetius opened the door a crack and peeked in, just in time to see Casca surface like a porpoise, catching a breath of air and then joyfully plunging back into the quivering mass of women, sinking into the best of all possible oceans. Closing the door quietly, Paetius mumbled wonderingly, "I just don't see what they get out of it." Shaking his head in sad confusion, he went back to the main room in time to break the arm of a Nubian who pulled a knife on a fellow Greek from Thessaly.

"I don't allow that shit in my place," he bellowed and tossed the Nubian into the street, fractured forearm and all, leaving him unconscious for the vigeles to find.

Casca woke to the pounding on his door, thinking for a moment that it was coming from inside his own head. His whole body ached and he hadn't felt this bad when he had been a gladiator in the arena at Rome. The pounding continued, "Just a moment," as he untangled himself from the mass of naked bodies that covered him, moving legs and arms out of the way. Slipping his tunic on he stumbled to the door and upon opening it, the portly form of Ortius stood leering from ear to ear, a pot of wine in his hand which he stuck under Casca's nose.

"My gods, no! Get that shit away from me!" His stomach performed a minor upheaval which he squelched with some difficulty.

"No? Then, I'll drink it myself." Ortius swallowed the cupful in one gulp and tossed the empty vessel into the room where it joined the pile of exhausted whores, who had done such noble duty. "Come my friend, a good breakfast of cold mutton is just what you need to fix you up."

The idea of eating cold grey mutton was too much for Casca and he barely made it to the chamber pot, having to throw several legs out of the way to get to it.

A couple of hours later, when he felt his heart was beginning to beat with some regularity and the blood had drained from his eyes, he thought he just might make it through the rest of the day. Ortius showed no effects at all from the night's bout of drinking and took Casca everywhere, constantly retelling the sea battle until their feats began to rival the gods of Holy Olympus. Dubrae was a thriving port and Roman culture was everywhere.

The next few days brought up-to-date the events which had been transpiring in the Empire since he had left Helsfjord and the Hold from which he and his two ships had set sail so long ago . . . or was it so long. Thinking carefully, he realized with a shock that it had been only four years since they set sail for the unknown and reached the lands of the Teotec where men were sacrificed on the altar to the gods. Quetza they had called him, the Serpent. Touching the scar on his chest, it seemed so much longer ago, but then time is a matter of happenings and never stays the same. To a man in pain, minutes seem hours; to lovers, there is never time enough.

The day came for Ortius to take ship and again leave the island of Britannia; he would make the long voyage past the Pillars of Hercules to the warmer waters of the Mediterranean. Would Casca sail with him?

The two had grown inordinately fond of each other in their time together and Casca readily agreed. What difference did it make where he spent his time? It must be spent somewhere and it had been too long since the warm winds of Italia had blown in his face.

"Aye, noble Captain, scourge of the Saxons, I will be pleased to sail with you again. Besides, should you not make it on your own, I would feel responsible. So we will ship together once more."

Ortius bellowed in joy and called for wine again. Casca laughed as the pots were brought. Paetius was saddened by the news they were leaving; he had never quite given up hope that he might show Casca the way to sincere love, the kind only men can know. Sighing, he watched the two head for the docks and a tear ran down one eye as he mentally composed a poem to commemorate the occasion of lovers parting. Ah well, at least his new friend from Thessaly would help ease the pain.

Four
RETURN

The single-banked trading galley of Ortius crept gingerly along the coast turning northwards to the first port of call, Nova Cargegena, then on to the Messina, where Casca had first enlisted in the legions and received his basic training. From there he had been sent to join the Seventh Legion in Gaul. Messina had not changed much. They still made the best fish stew in the Empire.

On the voyage, Casca often took his turn at the oars when the wind failed, falling into the rhythm of the stroke and beat that spoke of the years in the slave galleys of Rome. The exercise did him good and helped keep his arms and back strong and muscled. The sweat that flowed down into the hairs of his chest was welcome. Ortius was a good friend and would have had him do nothing but drink and eat and tell lies about their amorous adventures, but a man needs to work, to strain to be alive. At least now he rowed because he chose to. There was no cracking flash of pain from a slave master's lash to rip his back into shreds of hairline cuts. The nights were cool and Father Neptune smiled on them, keeping his storms away and sending only gentle winds to aid them on their way. The creaking of the planking served as a sirens' song to lull the mind and put the body to rest after a long day on the oars.

Somewhat to Casca's chagrin, Ortius promised him an even more fantastic night than the one he had had in Dubrae when they reached the port of Ostia. With Ortius, one could never be certain when the chubby little sailing master was going to do a number on you.

The wind was coming from Africa and the last days were spent tacking slowly back and forth with a greater amount of time spent using the oars, but at last they heard the call of the lookout.

"Ostia! Ostia lies ahead!"

Eagerly Casca climbed up the mast to join the lookout. The red tiled roofs and white buildings shimmered in the afternoon sun. He was almost there. The tide swept them into a smooth docking at the stone wharves of the gateway to Rome.

Leaping onto the wharf, Casca felt a rush of déjà vu, but knew it was memory of long ago when he first set foot on these very stones as the property of the patrician proconsul, M. Decimus Crespas, his owner and master who brought him to Rome to fight for the pleasure of the masses and jaded nobility. Now, as then, the city swarmed with life. Grain ships from Egypt and beyond, others like Ortius' stout trader came from Gaul or Brittania and across the straits of Sicilia from Carthage.

Ortius told Casca to stay put while he presented his papers to the cargo master, again using the tried and true method of honorable bribery to make sure his cargo was not too closely inspected. Bureaucrats were all the same.

While waiting, a squad of Legionaires marched by. To Casca's eye, they were disappointing; the troops in distant Dubrae looked much sharper. These were sloppy in their dress and manner; the old razor-sharp discipline of his day was vanishing. Even the uniforms were not all the same and two carried swords other than the Gladius Iberius, a sure sign of internal rot.

Ortius and Casca spent three days tasting the pleasures of Ostia and coming up-to-date on the happenings of the empire. It was not too good. Gallenius had been removed while they were at sea and the empire was in sad disorder on every frontier. The Legions had been pushed back until they held only central and southern Italia. Most of the north was ravaged at will by marauding bands of vandal Goths and any others who chose to rape and pillage. Gallenius had been replaced by two of his own calvary commanders, members of the equestrian order who quickly reduced the professional politicians to a state of abject obedience, Claudius and Aurelian.

The military had control of the empire. Whether it would do any good or not was yet to be seen, but for now, the generals ruled. Walking the streets of Ostia with Ortius on one side of him they ignored the pleadings of the whores to come in and be given endless delights for only a few coppers. They stopped in a wine ship that boasted a good collection of rare vintages from as far away as Parthia and Egypt; making their way to a table, they sat talking of the world and politics and, naturally, women.

Ortius still gloated over the gambit he pulled on Casca in Dubrae and fell into a fit of laughter when he related how Paetius had come to him, wounded to his soul, and described the death grip of the Egyptian whore on Casca's big toe, tears of laughter rolling down his cheeks until he fell into a coughing spasm and spilled the table over, knocking a couple of sailors off the stools next to them. The two tough looking Corsicans scrambled to their feet cursing and wiping a mess of spilled wine and food from their tunics. The shorter of the two reached over and gave Ortius an open-handed slap that knocked him to the floor, his face burning from the blow and head ringing where the man's hand popped his ear. Leaning over, the short man reached to grab the portly ship's master and pulled him up for another blow when a grip like steel wrapped itself around his wrist and froze him.

"Enough. It was an accident." Casca rose, trying to control the beginning surge of anger. The short sailor tried to twist out of the iron grip only to feel it tighten until he thought the bones would snap. Years on the galleys of Rome had given Casca a grip few in the world could equal. The pressure increased. . .

"Enough. Go back to your seat and we'll buy you another round."

Before the short man could voice his agreement, a stool smashed across Casca's back and spun him over a table to meet with a boot in the mouth. He felt his lip split, letting the warm salt taste of blood into his mouth.

So much for trying to be reasonable, thought Casca. With a bellow, he dived into the legs of the large sailor and drove him over three tables and onto the tavern floor. Quickly he was swarmed by half a dozen sailors, raining blows on him with everything from wine pots to table legs. His head ringing, he grabbed a table leg for himself and began swinging, roaring out, "*Odin*," a habit he had picked up in the northlands, and began to crack skulls and ribs, ignoring returning blows. He cleared an area around himself and Ortius who had now come to his senses and was bellowing in glee, begging Casca to let him at them. The stubby balding man had no lack of guts and threw himself into the center of the remaining sailors and was just as quickly knocked out and thrown back like an unwanted fish. The remaining three sailors rushed Casca and buried him beneath them, pounding and pummeling with their hands and feet. The tall one made the mistake of trying to grapple with Casca on the floor and came up screaming in agony. Casca had reached under his tunic and given the sailor's balls one long strong squeeze that ended all thoughts of further hostilities in the fellow's mind and also any idea he might have had about love making for the next couple of weeks. Jumping up, Casca made short work of the two remaining sailors with a snap kick to the throat of one and back knuckle to the temple of the other that dropped him like he was pole–axed.

Gathering Ortius up, he tossed him over his shoulder and backed his way out of the tavern and into the dark where he quickly lost himself in the maze of streets. Finally finding his way back to their rooms, he set about waking Ortius with a combination of wet rags and gentle slaps. The Sicilian came to swinging and nailed Casca a good shot in the eye which immediately swelled shut.

"Where are they?" he cried. "I'll teach them to mess with Ortius, the terror of the Saxon coast."

Another gentle slap put Ortius back into the land of Nod and Casca just looked at him, touched his sore eye and said piss on it. He hit the sack, but felt good. It had been a great fight and dear Paetius, he felt sure, would have approved of the love squeeze he had given the sailor's balls. Yes, indeed, Paetius would have envied him that moment.

Leaving Ortius to nurse his sore ear, the next day Casca told him he was going to Rome for awhile and that if he didn't get back before he sailed, then Hale and Farewell. The road had been good. Ortius was too sore and hung over to more than voice a feeble protest at his abandonment, but wished him well saying they sailed in two weeks for Byzantium if the weather permitted.

Casca left him holding his head between his hands vowing to forsake the worship of Dionysius and his grapes and devote himself to a life of piety and devotion. Paying his two coppers fare, Casca caught a ride in the morning on one of the wagons that hauled tourists and visitors to the capitol. It was early afternoon when they reached the outskirts of the city. Casca got off to walk the short distance to the school of the Galli where he had worn the armor of the Mirmillone and trained for the arena.

The walls were overgrown with vines and signs of

decay were obvious from a distance. Pushing open the gate, the rusted squeaking hinges welcomed him. Gone. All were gone. Only ghosts of the hundreds who learned the fine art of slaughter were left. Open doors and litter left by bands of beggars who occasionally stopped and lived for awhile in the school of slaughter were all that remained.

The chopping posts were still there, gouged and scarred from the endless line of men who chopped them for hours to strengthen their sword arms and as a light wind blew small whirlwinds of dust, Casca thought he could hear Corvu again cursing and correcting, calling to low strike for the gut, try it again; over and over, the dust whirled and in it he saw familiar faces. Crysos who had died for him and Jubala, the insane savage black from Numidia, who feasted on his victims. All were gone and only dust remained. Casca. The only one left.

His sword felt heavy on his belt, weighing more than he knew. Perhaps it was heavy with the lives of the men he sent to their gods and ancestors. Entering the small arena where private shows were held for the rich, he noted that weeds now grew in thick clumps in the remaining sand. Perhaps the blood of those who had fallen here gave them sustenance. Kicking a patch of weeds, melancholy swept over him with the wind in this sanctuary of death.

"I have lived so long with the stench of death that sometimes I cannot tell it from my own breath . . . or are they the same?"

Climbing the steps to the box where the rich would sit eating while the men below died for their pleasure, he could even hear the whisper of the roar of the crowd in the great arena of Rome. "*Iugula!*

Go for the jugular! Give it to him!"

Below, the forms of men swirled in his mind as they fought, a wounded Thraces, his winged helmet slashed open held up a finger to the crowd asking for mercy which was seldom given. Useless, useless. What purpose did it all serve? But there was an excitement. Perhaps it's the animal that lives in all of us. We know what we do is wrong but still when lust comes on us, we revel in our ability to triumph over one another, even though it serves no purpose in the end. Man, the fighter, the killer of his own kind as no other beast on the face of this world is. Sighing, Casca rose to make his way out of the haunted mausoleum.

We are what we are. He left the school and walked to the gates that would let him into the city of the Caesars.

Five
ROME

Casca's steps led him through the same paths that he had taken to fight against Jubala in the arena of the Circus Maximus. Guards at the gateway gave him no more than a cursory glance as he melted into the flow of humanity. The sounds and smells were the same as he remembered, a babble of all the tongues of the empire merged into one distinct sound.

Dark closed over the City of the Caesars. The poor and the workers were in their homes behind shuttered doors. Over a million people crowded into the warrens of the city, driven here by the constant raids of the barbarians to the north or the free dole of grain. The odor of crowded humanity was intense and the smell brought the aura of fear . . . a fear that comes when the unknown walks the streets outside your home. Thieves and murderers owned the night. Only in the sections reserved for the wealthy merchants and highborn could a man or woman leave his home in the night with any semblance of safety and even here, the vultures waited and would strike and fade back into the crowded tenements and alleys.

In doorways and under the arches of the city, young people grappled and sweated, making frantic love, trying to find a moment's release from the fears of the day and the struggle to survive. Hot and eager for anything that could give them relief, they coupled, oblivious of the stares of the passersby. Only the streets which catered to the tastes of those who had money to spend were lighted and patrolled by guards. The guards were made available through payoffs to the Commander of the Roman Garrison.

Whores of both sexes did a flourishing business. No sexual fantasy or deviation could not be satisfied if one could pay.

Casca ignored the pleas of whores and pimps, touts for taverns and others who offered the sickest of pleasures. Rome was rotting—the guts and pride of those who had made her great were being absorbed by leeches and parasites who fed on her weakened body.

"I may yet outlive the Empire. . ."

All that night Casca walked through the city; it had changed some since the burning. They used more brick but it was basically as before, just more crowded. He could see flickering flames of altar fires of the priests on the terraced, well-tended hills. The gods needed constant attention and reassurance.

He stopped outside one massive structure—the

Colosseum, built after he had been sent to the galleys. A monument to depravity and brutality.

The Colosseum was a huge oval, covering six acres with eighty entrances of precious marble facings. In it 40,000 people could indulge their senses in the meaningless slaughter of the helpless. The games had deteriorated to nothing more than that. There was no time for expert fighters to compete against each other; only a few aficionados appreciated the fine use of weapons. The masses wanted only blood. They delighted in the pain of those being torn apart by beasts or used as living torches to light the interior of the arena while old men were made to beat each other to death with clubs, the crowd roaring in laughter at their feeble efforts.

Several times he saw the mark of those calling themselves Christians scratched on walls and fences; somehow they seemed to be impossible to exterminate despite the best efforts of the Roman emperors who used them as scapegoats for every evil that befell the city. They continued to multiply and grow. Deep in the catacombs they held services and no matter how many were brought to the sands of the Colosseum or Circus Maximus, there were always plenty to be had later on for whatever special occasion might present itself.

Shaking his head in wonder, he grumbled to himself, drawing the curious looks of a couple of merchants being escorted by their private guards as they went to visit the district of whores.

How can a cult which preaches passivity survive when its followers are ruthlessly persecuted and killed, despised by everyone in power. Yet they continue to grow in numbers every day. Surely more people have died in the names of their gods than for any other purpose or reason. What good does it do?

The questions in his mind were too much for him to answer. Stopping to get a skin of wine, he made his way to the Tiber and sat on the banks wrapping his cloak about him and leaning back against a retaining wall. He watched the water and drank, washing the wine around his teeth and gums, feeling the cleansing quality of the vin ordinaire.

Several times he heard passersby laughing and quarreling, going to or coming from some form of pleasure. His mood was as black as the swirling waters that covered a thousand crimes. He felt a sense of loss, of betrayal. Rome had done nothing for him except to send him into slavery. Still, this was Rome, the only chance for stability the world had; without Rome civilization would be set back hundreds of years. What could take her place? Perhaps kindness would be a quick death rather than this lingering rot.

The grey of predawn crept slowly into the dark and drove the shadows back. Mists rose from the waters of the river and the barge men were readying their vessels for the day's labors. Slaves were preparing food in a thousand kitchens and babies suckled on their mother's breasts. Another day was coming, another day closer to the end which was surely approaching.

Grunting, he rose and pissed on a wall which he had been leaning against. He tossed the empty wineskin away and climbed back to the street leading to the Via Ostia.

Rome stank.

It was time to leave. There was nothing here for him.

He hitched his sword belt up a little higher, took a deep breath and with the mile-eating stride of the foot soldier, squared his back and marched down the deserted streets.

He had come, he had seen, and there was nothing here to conquer.

Rounding a corner past the temple of Claudius, he bumped into two men returning from their night's revels. Foul-mouthed and swaggering they cursed him for bumping into them. The loudest was a young man who still affected the close-cropped curled coiffure of the Julio-Claudian times. Facing Casca, the slender young man drew back an uncalloused hand and slapped Casca across the face.

Stunned for a moment, Casca did not move. He had been hit harder by sick children. Then his own hand responded in like manner, breaking the youngster's jaw, laying him out cold.

The young fop's companion stepped in front of Casca to bar his passage. This was no dilettante. The man had the look of blood about him. He stood approximately Casca's height and size with square shoulders. Close cut black hair hung to the nape of his neck and two silver bracelets encircled his thick and muscular wrists. Beneath the expensive cloak, Casca could see the hilt of a sword.

Confidently and arrogantly he pushed Casca back a step with an open palm.

"You really shouldn't have done that old boy. Now I'm going to have to put you in your place."

Tossing his cloak into the street, he stepped back drawing his blade, one a little longer than the old-fashioned Roman short sword Casca wore. "I see you are wearing a sword. Take it out and let's see if you can entertain me for a few moments."

The broad man made a couple of passes in the air with his blade, flickering the point under Casca's nose.

Sighing, Casca stepped back a pace and drew his own weapon. He tried to hold down his growing anger but the pulse in his temple increased its beat and his breath began coming in short spurts. He looked the other over, his grey-blue eyes black in the predawn light.

"I'll do my best to provide you with a little amusement. Now get it on, or get out of my way."

His opponent struck, expecting a quick kill, only to find his weapon blocked and an instant repartee that almost laid his guts open. He stepped back.

"Well, old boy, this may be better than I thought, but before I kill you, you should know you have the honor of dying at the hands of Marcellius Aelius."

He waited for the shock of his name to strike fear into the heart of this common trash that dared oppose him.

"Who gives a shit, you faggot."

Astounded at Casca's retort he said, "You mean you don't know who I am?"

"No, loudmouth, and frankly, I could care less. Now get on with it or get the hell out of my way. I won't tell you again."

Marcellius shook his head sadly. "So be it, you clod, but know this, I am the premier gladiator of Rome; I have fought and killed eighty-three times."

"Oh, fuck you," Casca swore and launched an

attack that left the other stunned and retreating. Casca's blade was a silver serpent, dashing and darting, flickering and flashing. He struck, beating the pride of the arena to the side of the temple wall. The man rallied and with a strong rush forced Casca back a couple of steps, then stood still breathing hard.

Fear was making its insidious way into his bowels. No one had ever done this to him.

Casca regained control of his temper. "Now, will you let me pass?"

Casca's question restored the other's confidence and he came on again with a high sweep that would have taken Casca's head off, only to feel a deep burning in his stomach. Astonished, he looked down to see Casca pulling the foot of the blade out of his gut. Still unbelieving he dropped his sword which clattered to the stones.

Casca wiped his blade off on Marcellius's cloak, looking at the fallen man squatting on the street holding his stomach, he gave a gentle shove with his foot.

"You amateur, you wouldn't have lasted three weeks at the school of Corvu. He would have fed you to the dogs."

The dying brain of Marcellius found time for one last wondering thought: "*Corvu?* He died over a hundred years ago. . ."

Six
BYZANTIUM

Casca stayed close to Ostia until the time for sailing. From Rome came the news of the death of the favorite of the masses—the glorius Marcellius—who had been set upon by at least ten thugs in the dark, according to his young companion who had his jaw smashed by a wicked blow from a club. According to the young gallant, Marcellius slew at least seven of the brutes before a blow from behind knocked him unconscious, whereupon the savages had finished him off and stolen away in the dark, taking their dead with them. It was indeed a tragedy for such a man to be struck down unfairly in the dark by thugs.

Ortius commented on the case as he read the daily report in the *acta diurnia*.

"I saw him fight a couple of times, Casca, old wart hog, and I do believe he might have given you a run for your money. But enough, we sail on the dawn tide. First port of call will be Naxos and then onto Carthage with a group of travelers and tourists. I made them a good rate on a package deal, but they supply their own meals. From Carthage, we cut back across, making stops at several other ports for whatever cargoes we can get and then on to Byzantium. Now, there was one hell of a city until Gallienus had the place sacked and looted. I used to know a couple of Armenian hookers—twin sisters they were—each would start at different points of your body and work their way to the center." Ortius sighed deeply and scratched his ass.

"Ahh! But I was younger then. It would probably kill me to try something like that now. Still a man is tempted to always recapture something of his youth, even if there is a price to pay. Is that not so, my overmuscled friend?"

Casca merely grunted noncommittedly and stuffed his face with fresh oysters from the bay. Rising, Ortius paid the bill and said, "I'm off for a massage and oiling. You finish up with the stevedores and make sure none of the bales are broken open."

They set sail with the dawn tide and were out to sea by the time the day broke in fully on them. The group of tourists going to Carthage immediately started chanting and wailing while they conducted a ritual among themselves. Words drifted up through the open hatch.

Casca was standing beside Ortius near the oar sweeps. Turning to him, he squinted as a beam of reflected light from the sea struck his face.

"They're Christians?"

Ortius nodded. "Aye, they're going to Carthage to escape. The word is out there will soon be another purge in Rome. In Carthage they are not bothered so much and even on occasions have been permitted to conduct their services openly. There are hundreds if not thousands there. Personally, I could care less what cult or gods they worship so long as their gold and silver is good. One thing about Christians—their god forbids them to cheat or lie." Laughing, he cleared his throat and spat phlegm over the side. "Did you ever hear anything so ridiculous in your life?"

After an uneventful trip, they docked at the inner harbor and tied up next to the storage houses used for transhipment of goods from the interior of the great African plains and mountains, most of which went to Rome.

The Christians were met by others of their sect and quickly left the harbor to find new homes and what they hoped would be safety from the coming persecutions.

Casca spent the day wandering through this miniature Rome where once the Carthaginians had challenged the power of Rome and were destroyed by the legions of Scipio. The city had resisted fanatically, the last survivors fighting to the death under the leadership of Hasdrubal in the Temple of Eshmun. With their death came also the death of the city as the conquerers pillaged and butchered. The stones of the buildings were broken and all human habitation of this place was forbidden on pain of death.

For twenty years only lizards and desert creatures lived in the rubble that once housed 700,000 men, women and children who were now no more. Mars is a vengeful god.

While Ortius attended to ship's business, Casca rented a piebald pony from a local stable and went for a tour of the city, glad to exchange the swaying of the ship for the bump of the saddle. On several walls he saw the symbols of old, of the hated gods of Carthage that the Romans detested so, for their savagery and rites of human sacrifice. Rome seemed to find no parallel between those who died in the name of a god and those sent to the arena to die for the amusement of the Romans. Casca wondered how the difference affected the enthusiasm of those to be killed. Passing a stone panel used to rebuild a wall enclosing the sumptuous *domus* of a retired senator who had taken up farming, he saw the emblems of Tanith, the supreme goddess of the city. Properly called *Tanit pene Baal*, the Other Face of Baal, the carving was that of the disk and crescent moon. The other face of Baal . . . the one he showed was bad enough.

Passing a market place, Casca saw a small bronze figure of the insatiable diety who demanded the firstborn of every family to be offered to him and fed to his flames. The small figure still held an aura of sinister depravity in the shape of human lips above the beard; crowning the figure were the horns of a beast.

Baal, Moloch, Jupiter, Quetza.

"Damn, what's the answer . . . what's the question?"

The African sun beat heavily on his back as he headed back to the wharves where ships lay in wait. Ortius was ready to put out to sea but had to wait for the tide on the morrow. That night was spent in a small inn near the waterfront. The morning found them cutting their way into the clear blue of the Mediterranean, heading northeast, carrying a new cargo of skins and ivory and amphorae of salted fish.

Casca cast one look back at the city founded by Queen Dido when she sought refuge on this hostile shore. It was said the king of the land offered her only the area that could be covered by the hide of a bull, but Dido (smart bitch that she was), held him to his word and cut the bullhide into thread-thin lengths and from this encircled the area that was to be her city.

The sea trail leading to Byzantium was marked by only a couple of minor storms. Two sailors and a pilgrim saw the shrine of Athena on one of the lesser islands of the group between Crete and Achea. Perhaps he should have been a devotee of Father Neptune or Poseidon as the Greeks knew him, but what's in a name—a god by any other name is still a pain in the ass.

At last with the coming of the summer solstice, they pulled into sight of Byzantium—nearly a thousand years old and founded by the Greeks, those great settlers of the Mediterranean world. Here, Casca knew his sea road would end.

Bidding a sad farewell to Ortius at the dock, he made his way through the streets which had not yet recovered from the ravages Gallenius had inflicted in order to squelch what he thought was a beginning insurrection. Across the straits lay Asia Minor, the gateway to the east. For some time now, the words of Shiu Lao Tze had haunted his dreams:

"Come to the East beyond the Indus."

Casca left Ortius tending to his usual condition of bribing the port officials and made a deal with a fisherman to get to the opposite shore across the propontis and land in the Asian city of Calchedon. From there he would begin his odyssey to the far east across the known lands of Cappadocia, Armenia, Media, Hyrcania and Parthia to the Oxus River, eighteen hundred miles as the crow or vulture flies. It would be next spring before he reached the frontiers of Bactria and from there he knew nothing of the way to Khitai, other than to head east, but others knew the way. In Rome itself, he had seen men of Shiu's race trading their cargoes of precious silk to the merchants of the city. The trail they took was called the Silk Road. Silk was smooth and soft, but Casca had the feeling this description would have nothing in common with the road he would ride. Securing the animals and supplies, he climbed into the saddle, tugging at the lead rope of his pack animal and headed out, out to whatever fate awaited him in the distance.

Ortius drowned his sorrow of the loss of his comrade by finding the twin sisters still in residence in the city—a little older and perhaps a trifle more shopworn then when he last saw them, but they had lost none of their enthusiasm for the trade of Aphrodite. They still knew how to work their way to the center of a man's attention and it had little to do with food. Casca was gone, but life went on. Ortius wished the Roman well and with the aid of the two sisters, drowned his sorrows with a rare vintage of 50-year-old Lesbos wine.

Seven
BROTHERHOOD OF THE LAMB

The flickering red glow of a distant flame told of the presence of men. Casca and the boy had seen no sign of life for the last two weeks. The limits of the Roman Empire were now far behind, past even the boundaries of the divine Alexander. The city of stone and mud-baked bricks that bore his name marked the end of his conquests. Here the Jaxartes River turned from the mountains to flow northward to the Aral Sea from the land of Han. From Eschate the Silk Road ran all the way to Rome, but there also was the wild country, filled only with danger for the unwary man or beast. Occasionally, roving bands of savages would sweep down from the steppes ravaging along the way, like monstrous locusts, leaving nothing in their path. Tarters, Huns and Mongols—along with lesser nations composed only of herds of horses, sheep and people: they were only a little better than their beasts and then only by the degree of cruelty they relished, that was unknown to the animals of the world.

As Casca wrapped his cloak closer about him, the scent of brush and dry air reached his nostrils. The slender form of Jugotai standing beside the pack horse stood out in marked contrast to this barren world of stones and rocky gorges. With every league into the wild lands, the boy seemed to grow taller. The closer they came to his tribal lands, the more his self-confidence increased. Fourteen years old as near as he could figure, he was a wild mop of black hair handing in a wind-swept mane to his shoulders, and anthracitic eyes. The chill of the night did not seem to bother him at all; indeed, he breathed more deeply, filling his chest with the dry wind.

During the weeks with Casca, he had already started to put some meat on his bones, especially those sticking out from his rib cage and chest. He was going home, to the lands of the Yueh-chih. The boy had been caught and sold by nomads when he was ten, to the placid farmers of Armenia for two copper pieces and a bent sword. The farmers being no match for the wild-spirited youngster, breathed a sigh of relief when he ran away, taking only a donkey for transport. The Hsuing-Nu forced his people out of the Kansu corridor 440 years before and forced the tribe to flee to Bactria for safety. Not until the time of the Emperor Wu Ti and his general, Pan Ch'oa, were the Yueh-chi able to build a nation known as the Kushan. This was their destination, the gateway to the wall that ran forever.

Though Jugotai's tribe was wild, they had been

heavily influenced by the envoys and trade with the Han Empire. They were also excellent horsemen, a fact easily demonstrated by Jogotai's ability to ride circles around Casca.

It was now time for the boy to return to his tribe. He was of the age to face the rites of manhood and nothing would stand in his way—save death itself.

The distant yapping of a pack of desert jackels came with the wind. The pack horse whinnied softly and was instantly quieted by his young master, a gentle hand and soothing hiss served to let the beast know all was well. Jugotai watched Casca with silent noncommittal eyes. The big man confused him. He had a blend of fierceness he had seldom seen equalled by the best of his tribe and a gentleness seen in some of the teachers who came to his people from the lamaseries to teach the words of Buddha.

With a nod, Casca indicated the path from the craggy hillside leading to the gorge where light was glowing and flickering. Ordinarily he would have bypassed the beckoning flame but as they were low on food and there was the chance the camp below might be friendly enough to barter for some of the silver denarii Casca had in the purse under his cloak, the two made their way down the hillside.

The horses picked their way gingerly through the rubble and stones, walking as if on eggs. The night was clear and lit by a full moon. As the distance between them and the fire closed, the wind shifted and the sound of chanting, bouncing gently off the basalt walls of the gorge was heard. Slowly the lines of a massive building carved out of living stone became visible. The chanting ceased before they could make out the words or the language. The glowing light seemed to be coming from the interior of the main building. The doors were opened wide and inviting, but Casca's hair prickled on the back of his neck, making him shift his sword to a handier position. Jugotai drew back and stopped out of sight from the range of the light. With a shake of his head he indicated he would go no further and pointed silently to the hillside to the east. Casca nodded his assent as the boy took the pack horse and faded into the gloom.

Watching him go, Casca thought, "Cautious little bastard, but maybe he knows more about this part of the world."

Dismounting, Casca lost his footing for a moment and almost fell. As he straightened, a soft whispery voice broke the silence as a hand came forward taking the reins of his horse.

"Welcome, we have been expecting you, Latin."

Regaining his balance, Casca took in the figure of his welcoming committee of one who spoke the language of Rome.

A tall thin figure in brown homespun robes reaching to the rocky floor of the gorge smiled at him. "Welcome," his host repeated. "I am Elder Dacort, the senior brother of this refuge for the lost and weary."

Casca looked at him, the hair on his neck still tingling. "How did you know I was coming?"

The man calling himself Elder Dacort laughed easily, his voice stronger than his appearance. "From the ridge you just crested to reach us. We could see you coming for a full day across the plains. This is the natural approach that one would follow after leaving the plains below. But where is your companion?" He looked about squinting at the darkness.

Casca shrugged. "Gone. After we reached the crest he decided to go on his own. No great loss. We were just traveling together for convenience, but all trails end sometime."

Elder Dacort smiled. "Yes, they do. They most certainly do. But enough of standing out here in the cold. Come inside and make yourself welcome. As you can see, there is no danger for you from such as we." He indicated his weaponless condition. Gently he took Casca's elbow and escorted him inside the confines of the building.

Casca still kept his sword at the ready. Then he saw the carvings on the door, the sign of the fish and the cross. He grumbled silently to himself, "Oh, no, not more Christians. At least I know they are harmless always preaching about steal not, kill not, and whatever else the Hades they can think of not to do."

Dacort noticed Casca's recognition of the symbols. "Yes, my brother, we are followers of the way of the gentle lamb. Here we study his words and preserve them. Our years are spent in quiet meditation and prayer for the salvation of the souls of the world." Escorting his guest to a side room from the hall lit with torches in iron brackets to a table laid with food and wine, he said: "You see we have been waiting for you. We cannot perform the miracles of our Lord Jesus and turn water into wine or make one loaf of bread feed thousands, but we do have some small fields not far from here that provide enough for the brotherhood and the few guests who come this way." He seated Casca at the head of a wooden table designed to seat some twenty or more, in a room projecting a feeling of great emptiness. Casca looked around, noting he had seen no one but Elder Dacort since entering the place.

Dacort observed Casca's look and replied, "The rest of the brotherhood are at rest or at prayers. We rise quite early to say our devotionals, then go to the fields." The smell of roast goat and fresh bread convinced Casca to sit. Elder Dacort handed him a plate piled high with food and sat watching. Casca started to take a drink of wine and then hesitated, putting the cup back on the table.

Dacort laughed gently and took the cup in his hands and drank. Smiling, he then ate a small portion of each of the foods on Casca's plate.

Casca smiled, embarrassed. Dacort halted his protestations with an up lifted palm. "No need for explanations my son, it is a cruel world and there are many pitfalls awaiting the unwary."

While Casca ate, Elder Dacort talked of Rome and the world. Casca found this gaunt man quite well informed on happenings in Rome, as well as what lay beyond to the east and other lands Casca had never heard of. The man's voice was soothing and soon Casca's limbs felt heavy, his eyes like leaden weights. He began to feel the first distant tinge of fear and tried to stand. His legs were like water. All the while, Dacort talked to him softly of the world and its happenings as if not noticing the wine being overturned and the wooden plates crashing to the floor as Casca fell, face first, into a left-over mess of goat and bread.

Dacort smiled to himself as he stood over the

sprawled out figure of the former legionary. Reaching into his robes, he took out a small vial in the shape of an amphora and took the remaining fluid with a grimace of distaste. "The antidote was bitter as green figs," he thought. "Prior planning pays off," he smiled as he had when he had dosed himself long before Casca's appearance at the steps of the Temple of the Lamb.

The next day, Casca lay as one dead to the world. His host and the rest of the brethren were preparing for the most holy day of their year. Prayers echoed throughout the halls and chambers. Soon it would be time.

Dacort trusted no other than himself to watch over his unconscious guest. Casca lay on a skin-framed cot wearing only his tunic, his sword on a shelf nearby. Dacort knew well the strength of his potion. The Roman would sleep for yet another day, but it paid to be careful. Administering another dose to his guest that would guarantee his remaining in a comatose condition for another twenty-four hours, Elder Dacort went to prepare himself for the great day ahead. Giving Casca one last look and satisfied that the man would remain as he was, the elder left.

Casca's mind filled with images leaping across and then fading, images of ships and pyramids, Saxons and Parthians, mountains and deserts. His stomach turned inside out, spewing out the fluids given him. Consciousness returned by millimeters, Head aching, he rose to his elbow and ran his tongue over his gums. "By Mithra, it tastes like a camel just shit in my mouth." His stomach turned again and the last of its contents spilled onto the stone floor. Weaving on unsteady legs, he rose trying to focus. His sword. Where was it?

Stumbling to the shelf, he held the blade in his hand and pulled it from its scabbard, the feel of the familiar grip restoring him. "Now I'll give those psalm-singing, drink-dopers something to pray about. They better pray I don't carve all of them into legs of lamb."

Breathing deeply through his mouth, he let his strength return. Shaking his head from side to side to clear the fog from it, he moved to the door. Raising the latch, he stuck his head out and glanced down the hall. The lamps in the iron brackets were out; cracks of bright light told him it was day outside.

"Where in the Hades are they? Is everyone here mad? What do I mean by everyone?" He stopped and thought, "The only bastard I've seen is that damned so-called Elder and that sucker certainly doesn't behave in a Christian manner. Where are they?"

Making his way on still unsteady legs, he held his short sword ready, wondering if Jugotai was still on the loose.

"Probably," thought Casca. "The little desert rat has more sense than I do."

The large door swung open on greased hinges and Casca slipped out looking to see if his horse was there. No luck. Staying close to the sides of the building, he kept to the shadows until he came close to a patch of boulders and brush. Bending low to the ground, he raced across and threw himself to the gravel behind the boulders leaving a skin mark running from his ankle to his knee.

He saw nothing. Only the dry wind whispered

through the brush and the rocks. It was close to midday. Crawling backwards, he kept his eye on the temple until he was certain he couldn't be seen from that direction and headed for high ground. If Jugotai was anywhere around, that's where he would find him.

Climbing over rocks and boulders, he reached a small plateau and there lay flat on his stomach, letting his gaze run over the countryside, searching for any sign of movement. As far as he could see from his aerial perch, there was nothing but the wild country and the temple in the gorge below.

"There! A movement." Wiping a trickle of sweat from his eyes, he saw something move again. One man and then another and another, all in brown robes, their hands moving and bodies twisting, came into view. The man in front was carrying something on his shoulders. A log? The trail made a turn and Casca started. The man in front was carrying a cross. Distant sounds reached him, but they were too far away to make out. Watching their direction, Casca looked ahead and picked up the trail where it reached a small mound. Working his way carefully, he sped ahead of the group and found a sheltered spot underneath some brush that also provided protection. From this spot he could see where the trail stopped. Settling himself down, he wished for water or anything to quench his thirst.

For now he would have to wait and hope Jugotai was nearby; if he was, then they would have to figure out what to do next, especially about Casca's horse.

Eight
THE GUARDIANS

The column of hooded figures wound its way to the place of fulfillment. The devotees whipped themselves and their brothers with flails of thorns and cried out in ecstasy, the pain a drug to bring them closer to God, filling them with the pain of Jesus. They were as one with him in his agony.

They cried and wailed in fanatic fervor. The fortunate one chosen to represent Jesus as they relived his last moments, was the most ecstatic of all. His eyes glazed, he frothed at the mouth and spoke in tongues as he labored under the weight of the cross he bore on his shoulders, the wreath of thorns stuck in his forehead let trickles of blood run their sticky course down his cheeks and clotted in the hairs of his thin beard.

God was with him. The spirit of Jesus walked with him. He knew the glory of the Messiah's pain.

Laboriously, he carried his instrument of death to the crest of the mount and there lay his burden down as his brethren begged him to forgive their sins and transgressions. Placing himself on the cross, he stretched his arms, resting them on the crossbeams, the feel of the rough wood on his skin sensual. He opened his eyes wide and screamed in pleasure, the knowledge of his certain salvation was manifest when the first spike was driven through the space between the wrist bones into the roughened wood of the cross; then again and once more he screamed as the last spike nailed his feet together. He cried out to the glory of the Lord God and to the honor that was his, to be able to experience all that the Lord Jesus did on this Holy of Holy days, to ascend and sit at the feet of the master, to be one with God himself.

His brethren whipped themselves even more, many laying their backs open to the bone. They wailed as the cross was set into place. The scenario was almost complete. The crucified supplicant prayed not to die before the allotted time had passed. He must feel every second and minute of the divine agony, until the final great moment which was yet to come.

The Guardians of the Blood of the Lamb threw back their hoods from their rough homespun cloaks, exposing tear-streaked faces in contorted caricatures of ecstasy as they wept for the Lamb.

"*Longinus,*" they began to chant, the name echoing from the nearby hills. "*Longinus.*" Over and over, in rhythm with their own heartbeats, they chanted.

Casca felt a shiver run over him as his name was

called. From his place of concealment, everything was visible; the bushes he was hiding behind served only to keep him from the eyes of the Guardians. But why were they calling his name?

The answer was not long in coming. Elder Dacort approached the crucified sobbing man, wearing the uniform of the legion of two hundred years ago, complete with trappings and insignia of the Legion, the Jerusalum Garrison. His red army cloak billowed in the wind, Casca noted that the Galdius Iberius was in the proper position on the priest's right side and then in the monk's left hand he saw the filum.

"*The spear, Longinus,*" the monks wailed. "Have mercy!"

Elder Dacort stood at the surrogate Christ's left side and raised the spear, his face wild, long beard whipping in the growing wind. Even from this distance, Casca could see the weapon clearly, His mark was on it, where in practice, a careless lunge had left a deep scar in the wooden haft running a foot up to the base of the metal blade.

"It's mine. It's my spear. Where did they get it, and how?"

The brother on the cross looked at his executioner in delirious pleasure. The time was near. Raising his eyes to the heavens he cried out, "O my father, why hast thou forsaken me," and shivered in pleasure.

As the mock Roman drove the spear into his side, some words were lost to Casca as the wind blew them away but several came through clear enough to make his stomach jerk in fear. . . "*As you are, so you shall remain. . .*"

The spear was withdrawn from the man's side

and blood poured forth, covering the weapon for a foot or more down the blade.

The brethren crawled on their bellies, moaning as they slid over the stones to the base of the cross, then rising up high enough to lick blood off the weapon and fall into a fit approaching a religious orgasm. Each in his turn, drank the blood of the crucified Lamb.

The blessed one on the cross shivered and died, his body hanging with limp arms outstretched at the shoulder sockets.

Elder Dacort in his Roman uniform held the spear above his head. Crying out, his voice almost a shriek: "Behold, the spear of Longinus, the spawn of Satan. Through the Blood of the Lamb, was he given life . . . life to walk the earth until the master returns. The founder of our order, Izram the Syrian, who came to join the master and became the thirteenth disciple, was at the Mount of Skulls and heard the words of the Lord Jesus that condemned the Roman dog to life. It was Izram who witnessed the blood of the Lamb touching the dog's tongue and thereby transforming him into the undying beast he is now and Izram who bought the Roman's spear from his comrades after the beast was sentenced to the mines. Izram founded our holy order and gave unto us the keeping of the most holy of relics, the instrument of our Lord's death . . . the spear of Longinus . . . Longinus, who must walk the earth until the master comes again. May his every moment be filled with pain unbearable, prolonged through the centuries; may worms nest in his eyes and rats live in his bowels. Longinus lives through the blood of the Lamb as we shall live in Paradise through the blood of our blessed martyred brother, who has become one with the Lord Jesus. Behold the spear of the murderer, the holiest relic in our world, the gateway to heaven."

His eyes flashed as he waved the weapon above his head. "Brothers, pray with me and curse the name of Longinus, the *Killer of God!*"

The brethren cried tears of agony, which flowed into the dry ground and mingled with the blood of their self-inflicted wounds where they had scourged themselves. They moaned and sobbed crying out, "*Longinus, Longinus, Longinus. . . .*"

Taking the body of their brother from the cross they washed and cleansed it and reverently carried it away sobbing; the act was complete. Elder Dacort disappeared from sight while Casca watched the others at their grisly chore.

Moving from his place of concealment, he worked his way back to the shrine area and the main temple. Sand in his sandals gritted against his skin, giving him the feeling of walking on needles. Dark was coming and the horizon was bathed in a red glow that gave him the feeling of being immersed in a strange aura.

No one was present. No disciples were to be seen. Only silence, the silence of the Asian wind, blowing into the interior and whispering against the cut stone wall making the torches in their brackets dance and sway. Instinctively staying close to the side of the hall, Casca moved down the corridors following the trail of lit torches to the inner sanctum of the Brothers of the Blood of the Lamb. He could now hear clearly the singing and chanting and fanatical preaching of Elder Dacort. "It must be here . . . my spear," he thought. He knew the best action he could take would be to place as much distance between himself and these fanatics as possible, but a compulsion to see the weapon closer drove him on.

Stopping at the door, he listened for any sign of life inside. Hearing nothing, he carefully drew his sword and opened the massive doors engraved with stylized emblems of the fish and crucifix. Slipping in, he closed the door behind him facing the interior, a room of not more than forty feet wide but over two hundred feet long. The stones were polished smooth from the endless tread of bare feet and knees crawling over them in supplication to reach the sacred object enshrined over the carved wooden representation of Jesus crucified. The spear, no other ornamentation was there, only bare stones which seemed to amplify the pleadings of the loyal followers of Izram, the thirteenth disciple.

Walking as if hypnotized, he saw only the spear before him, drawing him like a magnet; here was the beginning and ending of his life. His sword grip grew sweaty in his right hand and the blade increased in weight with every step, the sound of his own heart beating drummed in his ears like thunder, his breath began to come in short gasps and his feet became as lead.

The spear drew him until after what seemed like an eternity, he stood before it. The face of the crucified Christ seemed to mock him. The brass spikes through the wrists made Casca's own wrists ache as if they too were nailed to the cross. Light from the torches bounced off the spearhead, revealing traces of blood still visible, having dried to a dark stain on the blade and shaft. The spear rested on a silver bracket over the Christ. Climbing the three steps, his left hand went out slowly and fearfully, reaching, his fingers shaking.

"My spear, almost three hundred years and it is here," his fingers touched the wooden shaft and like of old, they gripped the weapon and lifted it from the silver brackets, his eyes never leaving the blade. The shaft seemed to twist and squirm in his hand, or was it his own trembling that seemed to give the weapon a life of its own? Casca's lips formed one soundless word: "*Mine.*"

A blinding flash of pain and darkness claimed him . . .

Elder Dacort stood over Casca's body and motioned the brother with the club to move back, and bending over, took the spear from the fingers of the killer of his God and reverently placed it back into the silver bracket.

Smiling to himself, the Elder Dacort had Casca carried from the sanctuary to a smaller room to the left of the main hall and laid him on the floor after first taking his weapon and placing it in a cupboard. He then sat and waited, his blood-flecked eyes never leaving the Roman's face.

Content to wait, for after all, they had waited for the last three centuries, what matter a few more moments. For three centuries they had been waiting at this, the only bastion of the true faith. Every stone had been made by the hands of the brotherhood. They knew their duty, to keep the true faith of God. Only a chosen few were recruited to take the place of those who died, either by infirmity, accident, age or were blessed enough to take the supreme part of the act of Golgotha.

Dacort stroked his thin beard with gnarled fingers, the nails worn down to the meat from the hours he had spent on his knees scrubbing the floors of the sanctuary. The Roman uniform was back in its place, waiting for the next holy day; now, like the others, he wore his robe of homespun rough brown wool.

Casca stirred. Elder Dacort clapped his hands and two brothers appeared dressed the same as he, carrying a length of timber. They tied Casca's arms to it keeping them outstretched. Dacort would take no chances. The Roman heretic was dangerous and must not escape his punishment.

Casca awoke, his head throbbing, spots flashing before him, until his eyes finally focused upon the Elder smiling at him from his chair. Trying to rise, Casca fell back, noting for the first time that his arms were tied.

Dacort motioned for the two brothers to raise him to the kneeling position, one on each side, they obeyed. Almost gently, they placed Casca on his knees before the Elder. The elder rose. Standing gaunt and skeletal, his whole demeanor was that of a man with a sacred mission.

Pointing his finger at Casca, he said: "We have waited long for you to come, Casca Rufio Longinus."

Casca jerked.

"Yes, we know you and know you well. Through the ages you have been watched. When you slaved in the mines of Greece those long years, Brothers of the Lamb were there; when one died, another was sent to take his place. In the arena, the men who served your food were of our order, even on the benches of the warships of Rome we were there. We lost you for a time when your ship wrecked on the shores of Greece, but found you again in Parthia;

lost yet again when you crossed the Rhine, but we knew you would return. Always we have waited and now, Praise the Lamb! You are here." Dacort's voice almost a whisper, he hissed: "You are the greatest defilement to ever exist, you are an abomination, but you are the road that leads to God. Jesus said to you . . . As I go now to my father you must one day come to me . . . you are the trail that will lead one day to the coming of the Messiah and we shall be there with you. We know you, Casca Longinus, better than you know yourself. We will not try to kill you after all; we both know it would be useless and neither shall we confine you, for how else can you lead us to Jesus?"

"No, spawn of Baal, you must go free, but you shall be punished. You dared to touch the most sacred relic with your filthy hand. You performed the sacrilege and as the word says, '. . . if thine eye offends thee, cast it out . . .' surely that must also apply to other portions of the body."

The hatred in Dacort's voice washed over him: "Thy hand offends *me*!"

Swifter than Casca would have believed the elder capable of moving, he saw the flash of an axe come from the elder's robes and cold burning as the blade of the axe sunk into the wood of the cross beam. There was a dull thump and Casca looked down to see his hand lying in front of him on the stone floor, draining. Then the pain began and Casca screamed as the stump of his wrist was washed in the flames of a torch held by one of the brothers, the smell of his own cooking flesh, clotted in his nostrils and the dark took him once more, mercifully.

Nine
JUGOTAI

The Brothers of the Lamb tossed Casca's unconscious body on the rocks, tying his horse to the brush nearby. A fly walked over his eyelids, sucking up the salt moisture that had collected there and then, satisfied, flew off.

Elder Dacort stood alone, looking down at what to him was the vilest piece of filth the world had ever known. Reaching into a pocket from under his robes, he withdrew the claw-like stump of Casca's hand. Throwing it to the ground, he spat upon Casca's unconscious body.

Dacort walked slowly down the hillside, his sandals kicking up small clouds of dust, his head bowed and handed folded together, and prayed.

Casca woke to the throbbing in his wrist. Squirming he tried to fight his way back to awareness. The pain burned and spread up his arm.

"I can't move . . . why can't I move?"

A jolt brought his eyes open. He was tied to the saddle of his horse. In front, the small wiry form of Jugotai was leading the horse. Casca tried to take the reins in his left hand and felt awkward when he felt the fingers move, but nothing happened. Looking down, the sight of the seared stump brought it all back.

"*Those bastards have cut my hand off!*"

Indignation followed by anger which faded as another jolt bumped his stump against the side of the horse brought an involuntary groan. Jugotai's head turned.

Stopping the horses, Jugotai unstrapped Casca and eased him to the ground, taking his own jacket of goatskin, he made a pillow for the Roman's head and laid him down. Taking his skin of water, he washed Casca's face and let a few drops fall into the mouth slowly; too much water when a man has been wounded could make him worse . . . this his father had told him.

Casca slept again, this time quietly.

When he next awoke, the glow of a small smokeless fire warmed his face. Jugotai sat quietly watching, squatting on his heels as he had seen the sage, Shiu Lao Tze do many times.

"How do you feel?" The boy's voice was beginning to deepen and become a man's, Casca noted.

Groaning, Casca raised himself on his good arm. "How the Hades do you think I feel? I feel like shit, that's how."

Nodding, the boy smiled showing strong white teeth.

"Good, if you feel that way, then you're not too bad off."

Reaching into his travel bag, the boy took out Casca's hand and laid it on the saddle blanket which he squatted on. "What do you want me to do with this?"

The sight of his own hand lying there, fingers like claws reaching up, looking out of place and much too small to be his hand, as if the blood that had drained, left the member shrunken and undersized, gave rise to a feeling of nausea in Casca. He cleared his throat before speaking, "Give me a drink first."

Taking a long pull at the skin waterbag, the water tasted flat and warm, but good and eased the fire in his throat. Reaching over, he held the hand, the feeling of his own limp tissue sending chills racing over him. The hand was warm . . . warm to the touch.

Jugotai took a drink from the bag watching Casca. "I noticed that too. Do you want to tell me about it? Why is the hand warm when it should be cold and dead?"

Casca shook his head, "Later. Right now I have to think." I need my hand, I wonder . . . like the boy said, it's still alive. I have heard about some people having their ears sewn back after being cut off . . . perhaps . . .

"Sew it back on."

Jugotai stared for a moment and then went to the saddle bags to take out the bronze needle and threads of sinew he carried. Under the direction of the Roman, Jugotai lined up the severed piece making sure the bones matched. As the severed pieces rested on a flat stone on the blanket, he quickly ran a neat line of sutures around the entire wound, more often than not the needle would stick in the tough skin and he would have to twist and push to get it through, but the pain was nothing to the man he worked on. It was done. The stitches stuck out in knots where they were tied, but the hand was attached, though as yet gave no indication of wanting to return to work.

Tearing a piece from his cloak, Casca made a sling and put his hand to rest in it, out of sight. Another swallow of tepid water. Casca sighed, the burning was easing and the pain fading; back again but not beating at him. Lying down he looked up at the stars that were beginning to make their appearance in the night sky.

Finally he spoke. "It's a long story Jugotai. Let's just say that those men and I have had a bit of a difference over a religious matter and they took offense. As to my hand, we will just have to wait and see."

Casca told Jugotai about the ears he had seen sewn back on. His explanation seemed to satisfy the boy—for now anyway. Jugotai placed some brush on the small blaze, curled up in his blanket and slept. Dawn would come soon enough and the land of his fathers was still a long way off.

The next days they spent slowly climbing to higher ground. Water became more abundant as did game. It was seldom that Jugotai missed bringing back some game; small or large, antelope or hares, so long as it was meat, it made no difference at all to the two. High above them they could see snow on the peaks.

Several times every day, Casca looked at his hand and tried to will the fingers to move. Nothing. But the hand had not shown any sign of decay. They rode on.

On several occasions they saw large caravans in

the distance with strange two-humped camels. They rode and marched through an unending labyrinth of valleys and gorges, climbed mountain passes where the icy wind tried to cut them as though with cold knives. Climbing one icy overhang, Casca's horse stumbled and threw him to the ground. Slipping and sliding on the ice to the edge of a precipice, he reached out and caught at a twisted tree root and held on, pulling himself to a safe footing.

"I used my hand," he realized excitedly. His left hand had gone out involuntarily and grasped the twisted root of the tree, but now the hand would not let go. He pried the fingers open with his right hand and sat down, letting the wind whip at him, unmindful of the ice forming in his growing beard.

Crossing his legs, he squatted on the ice and stared at the hand, willing the fingers to move again. The forefinger gave one slight, almost unnoticeable twitch. Casca concentrated even harder, brows furrowed, unmindful of the cold sweat forming on his forehead turning to frozen crystals before it could run down his face.

The whole hand clenched, then opened again and clenched once more. Jugotai arrived on the scene in time to witness the act; saying nothing he pointed to the skies. Heavy dark clouds were racing overhead. A storm was coming. They must find shelter before the night.

Jugotai wasted nothing. He would gather the horses' droppings and save them, putting them into a bag to dry. When dried, they made an excellent fire in these high altitudes where there was a shortage of wood. Only the twisted dwarf trees stubbornly tried to find sustenance among the rocks, some sinking their roots twice and even three times their surface height into the ground, searching and seeking nourishment in the thin soil.

The storm hit with the force of a hurricane, seeking every inch of the cave they had taken for shelter. The horses in the rear whinnied and stomped their hooves as if they could feel the elemental forces that tried to rip off the skin coverings of the entrance. Four days the winds raged and screamed like mad women as the two sat in their rocky shelter. The remains of old fires told them this small haven had been a sanctuary more than once to the few travelers who ventured over the range.

"How much further?" Casca grumbled through his beard, while gnawing on a piece of mountain sheep Jugotai had nailed with a well-placed arrow six days earlier.

"Damn that's tough. You would think falling four hundred feet down on the rocks would have tenderized this sucker a little bit."

"How much further?" Casca repeated a little irritably.

Jugotai merely smiled and drew a rough map on the floor of the cave using his forefinger for a marker. "We are here. When we come off the mountain it will be but one day's ride to the boundaries of my tribe. From that time on, we will be watched and met when they decide to check us out. Perhaps five more days. Then beyond the next range of mountains lies the lands of the Han, or Chin. The land takes the name from whatever dynasty rules. Who sits now in the throne I do not know."

The storm left, leaving the bright clear sky and

air that only the highlands of the world ever know. Sharp and crystal-clear, the sun cast sparkles of myriad diamond-like beams from the ice and snow left behind by the Father of Winds, as Jugotai said the storm was called.

The trail to the valleys below was uneventful. When they gained the lower elevations, the horses found plenty of fodder on which to feed and stuffed themselves after the short rations on the heights above. Green fields of grass and full-sized trees greeted them. The smell of the rich earth and warm breezes was welcome and they removed their heavy blankets and skins.

Casca headed for the nearest pond, stripped and dived in, coming out just as quickly from the pond fed by the ice lakes of the heights. Steeling himself, he went in again, but more slowly this time, cursing with each step. He used sand to rub the grime of the weeks on the trail from his body. Taking his dagger, he honed it against his boot leather and scraped the beard from his face accompanied by an occasional grunt of pain and a curse. The job completed, he rinsed his clothes and set them to dry on nearby tree branches.

Jugotai looked at Casca as if he were utterly mad, but said nothing. He would wait until they crested the next rise to wash . . . where the hot springs were. Had he not told Casca of them?

Jugotai lay back to catch a nap while the horses ate and rested. Rolling over, he put his face into the grass and breathed deeply. The land of his fathers . . . he was here. Soon he would be a man, entitled to wear the curved sword and shave his head, leaving only one long lock to show all that here was a man ready to take a wife.

Ten
KUSHAN

Casca was still pissed at Jugotai for not telling him of the hot springs and was relating his displeasure to the youngster's obvious amusement, when an arrow buried itself into the limb of the juniper under which they were sitting while giving their beasts a break. Turning to Jugotai, Casca observed dryly, "I think your cousins have arrived."

Jugotai rose in his saddle and called out in a tongue Casca was unfamiliar with, though it was reminiscent of the tones Shiu Lao Tze used when he got excited—which had not been often.

"Peace brothers, I am Jugotai, son of Chu Shan of the Tribe of Kitolo, come home. This is my friend and travel companion. Be not disturbed by his appearance. He is not deformed. All from his lands have such big noses and red skins."

The unseen warriors came out of the conifer

treeline some three-hundred yards away. Casca whistled between his teeth. "That's one damned fine bow shot."

The riders galloped up closer while several kept their distance, bows ready. They were sturdy, well-muscled and of compact build with the look of men who took their calling seriously. Most wore hides of sheepskin with the wooly side out, though several had armor resembling that of the Parthian bronze-scaled jazerins and helmets of conical steel rimmed with fur. Their faces were dark from years in the sun and wind. Curved swords hung in leather scabbards with brass and bronze fittings. Their leader rode closer to speak with Jugotai. A black mustache hung below the chin of this man who appeared to be nothing but a mass of wiry knotted muscles, grafted to his horse's back.

Many questions followed with much head bobbing and gesturing. Finally the leader smiled and thumped Jugotai on the shoulder, then called his men who formed an escort on either side as indicated by him with his sword.

Five days they rode across the plains and valleys. They spotted many packs of wolves and once a spotted leopard who took off for higher ground when the riders thundered around a bend in a gorge. Villages dotted the countryside. These were strong people with great pride. Every man was a warrior if he was able to sit in a saddle.

On the dawn of the fifth day they reached their destination, a city lying in the valley between two huge mountains. A deep river came from the east, turned south to where it was joined by another from the west. At this juncture, the city lay in the basin.

The leader of the warriors noticed Casca's wandering eye and pointed to the river from the west. "Kabul." And then to the one from the east. "The Indus."

The great rocky pass they passed through served as a natural barrier to any attackers who would have to fight their way through the wild tribes charged with the security of the valley. Many of them had blue eyes and sunstreaked hair, almost blond, a striking contrast to their swarthy complexions. Several times Casca heard what sounded like Greek words mixed with the native dialects.

Jugotai told him many of the people were descendants of the soldiers of Alexander the Great after the Greeks conquered them. They still held they were superior to any other peoples because of their now fading bloodlines. No one had ever completely dominated them; the best kings could do was to make treaties with these people—they left the canyons and mountains alone in exchange for their guarding the mountain reaches against any invaders.

The pass was 80 miles from the junction of the river. The countryside reeked of poverty and hardships. In contrast, the city they entered showed great refinement and culture, the people were well dressed and the markets full of goods and food. Such was the way it had always been.

They entered through a massive gate that could be closed instantly if the ropes holding the gate to the winches were cut. Three axemen stood ready at all times to do just that. Soldiers were in evidence everywhere. In the city they wore more uniform clothing and had the look of professionals about them in comparison to the wild horsemen who escorted Casca and Jugotai.

Nishka, the warrior leader, called out to the guard commanding the approach to the city. Instantly an armed escort was provided to guide them through winding streets, past vendors' stands and workers in brass and gold. They passed statues carved in the hillside of a huge man, slightly fat with a placid look on his face and long dangling earlobes. Jugotai pointed to one of them: "Buddha."

The escort motioned them to dismount at the steps of the palace where a new escort was obtained after questioning the city guards and the hill tribesmen. Walking past a line of more smiling stone Buddhas they passed through one hall after another until they were shown into the presence of a man of obvious importance.

As they entered, Jugotai performed kowtow while Casca took a good look at their host seated behind a beautiful table carved of ebony and inlaid with scenes of great workmanship. The entire table glistened with fine lacquers of black and gold.

Tsin-tai, first secretary to the King of Kushan, Kidara III, was familiar. He was of the race of Shiu Lao Tze. His movements and the grace of his manner as he dismissed the palace guards again reminded Casca of Shiu Lao Tze. He had the same indefinable age of Shiu Lao, his face a wreath of gentle wrinkles. Overlooking Casca's lack of courtesy, he spoke first to Jugotai. His dark eyes sparkled when Casca's name was mentioned in Jugotai's story of their journey and difficulty in reaching Kushan.

The counselor motioned with a graceful sweep of his hand for Casca to be seated while he finished his questions. Food was brought. Most of the fowl was familiar and there was what looked like beef along with a thin chalky wine.

By the time the meal was finished Tsin-ta'i had given Jugotai permission to go with the servant but motioned for Casca to remain. Jugotai showed no sign of anxiety at this as Casca remained sitting until the counselor had regained his chair.

Playing with a large ring of intricately carved stone of pale green coloring on his finger, he spoke: "*Ave* Roman, welcome to Kushan." Laughing gently at Casca's shock at hearing Latin spóken, he explained, "We are not so far distant that some travelers do reach us from time to time. Always the restless ones, the searchers or the driven. Which are you, my big-nosed friend?"

Casca smiled, the ice broken with the familiar title Shiu Lao had given him many times, bringing a warm remembrance of his teacher whom this man in the blue silk robes so resembled.

The counselor continued. "The boy Jugotai will have what he wishes and be sent to his tribe in the south where he will become a man and enter the warrior class. As for you, how may we be of service? It is the way of the Buddha that travelers must be given aid and shelter as was he. To those our friends, we are welcome hosts, to our enemies we are what we must be. Regretfully, we cannot always respond in a gentle manner. But for you, who have returned a son to us, we are grateful. I feel the boy will grow into a man of importance one day; already he has shown great courage and now, if he learns wisdom, he will be of value to the Empire. Men of both courage and wisdom are scarce and must be treasured."

Thinking this over, Casca answered slowly. "Long ago I met a man from a place he called Khitai beyond the Indus. He said that one day I should go there. Perhaps as you said earlier, I am one of the driven. I have reached the Indus and now must go to Khitai, wherever that is."

Tsin-ta'i smiled and took a sip of wine from his lacquered cup. "What was the name of the man who told you this?"

"Shiu Lao Tze."

Tsin-ta'i stopped in mid-swallow. "Shiu Lao Tze?"

Casca nodded. "Yes, lord."

Tsin sat silent for a moment holding his fingers together, the points of his polished nails touching his chin. Then he spoke softly. "Shiu Lao Tze died over two hundred years ago. He was a great teacher and gentle man. I would not like to think you are using a name you picked up on the road frivolously." The warning was thinly veiled.

Rising, the counselor indicated that Casca was to follow him and led him out of the room and deep into the interior of the palace down into the cellars carved from the mountain.

Guards became fewer as they progressed until finally there were none at all to be seen. Shiu led Casca into a room lit with oil lamps, a library filled with scrolls and documents, many of which were sheepskin and even a large number of Egyptian papyrus. Tsin quickly scanned the markings on a number of scrolls and then selected one.

He unrolled the parchment carefully, almost reverently. "Roman, this is the chronicles of the travels of the sage Shiu Lao Tze." Placing the parchment on the table, he quickly scanned the rolls. Sucking his teeth, he turned to Casca. "What is your full name?"

"Casca Rufio Longinus."

Sighing, Tsin set the scroll aside and rubbed his eyes. "Turn your face," he ordered and held the lamp up to see better. "Yes, the scar is there. Sit down, Roman."

Casca did as he was bade, opposite the counselor.

Tsin pointed to the scrolls. "Your story is there. When Shiu Lao returned to his homeland after many years among the barbarians, he spent three years here, teaching. In that time, he wrote the story of all he had seen and experienced. His story of the Roman soldier condemned to live by the Jew called Jesus we took to be but the wanderings of the aged mind. But you are here, and if you are who you say you are, then it is indeed a wonder. The ways of the gods are inscrutable and we can only play the part our fate dictates. I believe the best thing I can to is to help you on your way, but not to Khitai as you wish to go. Khitai is where Shiu Lao Tze was born and lived as a child, but the land of his father's birth, and where he studied, is now known as the Chin. Before it was known as the kingdom of the Han dynasty but has since been broken into warring nations—the two most important, eastern and western Chin—it is to the western Chin you want to go. Now, we will find a suitable place for you and will talk more of what must be done to speed you on your way. The problems you present are more than I can deal with; I am not the great scholar and teacher that Shiu Lao was, only a poor bureaucrat. In the land of Chin, you will find scholars and wiser men than myself."

Taking the scrolls he led Casca back through the labyrinth of passages to his offices. Casca was turned over to the palace major-domo and shown to the rooms that would serve him for the time he remained in Kushan.

Eleven
ROAD TO THE WALL

Tsin-ta'i welcomed his guest and made him comfortable. With his own hand, he poured *tcha* and then dismissed all others, leaving the two of them alone. "I have thought the last two weeks on your plight and desires and feel that my original inclinations were correct. It is best for me to help you on your way. But before you go, it should be understood what you are going to and know something of the people of whom I am honored to be counted, though here I serve the Lord of Khosun."

From beneath the rosewood table, Tsin took a scroll like the ones Casca had seen in the dungeon library, and carefully laid it on the table.

"These are the writings of the scholar and historian, Ssu-ma Ch'ien. Over four hundred years ago, one Chang Ch'ien was sent by the Emperor, Wu Ti, to negotiate an alliance with a far tribe living beyond the boundaries of the Hsuing-nu. He was captured along with his servant and spent ten years as prisoner of the Hsuing-nu. After escaping, he made his way to this very place. Here he found the Yueh-chih who had been driven from their homelands by the Hsuing-nu and taken this place for their own. When the Yueh-chih came to this land, they first conquered Bactria, which still held to much of the culture of the Greeks, even to their art and writings. Here he found friends. To the south were other great nations not known to the people of Chin. Here too, he found goods from the southern provinces of the Empire of Wu Ti. The lands from which these goods came was then called the Shen-tu, far to the south and east where the inhabitants go to battle on elephants and live along a great river. For this information, he and his servant were honored. Though their original mission to make a treaty with enemies of the Hsuing-nu had failed, he found here other friends and the news that there was a great land close to the southern provinces. Chang Ch'ien was given high office. Even his faithful servant was rewarded with the title of Lord Who Carries Out His Mission.

"After leaving here, Chang Ch'ien was once more captured by the Hsuing-nu, but this time was able to escape after only a year's captivity and finally made his way to the Jade Gate, which guards the western end of the Wall from barbarism. The scholar Ssu-ma includes a description of that route and that is the one I think you should take. There is another route—the Silk Road runs all the way to the markets of the west—but to reach it from here would take you far back to the north. Taking the route of Chang Ch'ien, you will intercept the road at Ho-T'ien on the southern margin of the Tarim basin. An oasis is there that has given the city wealth and its placement on the Silk Road will supply you with more current information as to what is occurring in the Empire. A point of interest—Ho-T'ien is fed by two rivers which descend to the basin from the Kunlun mountains. They form one river and then join and disappear into the sands of Tkla-Makan except for a couple of months when it may reach the Tarim river if the season has been sufficiently wet."

Taking yet another scroll from beneath the table, Tsin laid it carefully out, using a couple of alabaster ink pots to hold the ends down.

"This is the map of the way to the Jade Gate."

The map was exquisitely drawn, the work of a master—the high and low regions were in different colors as were the rivers and deserts. Tsin pointed one polished nail to a spot on the chart.

"We are here. The Indus comes from the north and that will be the beginning for you. Follow the Indus. You will go through great gorges and valleys and the way will be difficult many times, but keep the river always to your right. The Indus will turn south again when you see the great peaks of the Naga Parat rising above all others. To reach the clouds, go another three hundred miles march and the Indus will then be joined by the Panglong Shoa. Follow the Panglong Shoa which will be the branch on the north for another one hundred miles and you will reach the trail leading north through the Karakoran pass and thence to the last of the mountain passes before you descend to the Tarim. Suget pass will be the final marker that you have left the highlands behind and will soon reach the Silk Road. You will know when you are on it by the bones of those who failed to survive the trek. Turn to the east once more and in three days you will reach Ho-T'ien. From there, the way is well known and you will have no trouble reaching the Jade Gate."

The exquisitely drawn scroll attracted Casca like a magnet. The beautifully drawn mountain ranges and rivers seemed to sweep him up into them.

"How far to the Jade Gate?"

Tsin looked at the border of the map and the confused squigglings that made up the writing of this people. "Something over two thousand miles."

"When do I leave?"

Tsin grinned gently. "Even now your animals are being prepared and supplies gathered. In the morning you will leave and to tell you the truth, I will be glad to see you go. I have the feeling that trouble is never far behind your steps and we have enough of that here already with the Hsuing-nu pushing from the north and the savage tribes to the south. It may be that our days are numbered already. If that is so, I feel no need to rush them by having you remain here any longer than necessary. Nothing personal you understand, just good business."

"I will have a simpler form of this map prepared for you to aid you in your travels and letters to the Emperor which will give you messenger status. Now, I have the business of the Empire to attend to."

Returning to his rooms, Casca sat on his bed and went over his gear, such as it was. He needed little and any extra weight from luxury items would not serve him on the trail. Back to basics: weapons, food and clothing. Nothing more. The nights would be cold but the sheepskins would serve to cut out the icy wind. Two thousand miles.

"Good enough. I have gone much farther than that already. I wonder if those crazy bastards from the Brotherhood are around." His wrist twinged at the remembrance.

Taking his horse and pack animal through the gate, he rode out onto the plain in front of the city of Kush. Casca crossed the bridge of wood and rope that spanned the Indus. There he gave one long look back, then settled his ass firmly in the saddle with the knowledge that he had a long way to go. A distant sound came to him from the rear.

Turning to look back, he saw a figure coming after him over the swaying suspension bridge. Reaching the solid footing of the opposite bank, Jugotai yelled to Casca to wait. The boy rode like a devil, swinging from one side of his horse to the other, swooping down to pull clumps of grass from the ground and then sliding under his horse's belly to appear on the other side and back into his saddle.

"That little bastard can really ride," Casca thought. "But that is the ugliest horse I have ever seen."

Jugotai's mount stood only about eleven hands and was covered with shaggy matted hair that dropped in clumps where he was losing his winter coat. The beast was as common looking as a pariah dog. Jugotai's head was clean-shaven save for the long scalp lock swinging behind him.

The curved blade swinging at his side meant business, not play.

"Ho, Roman," he called as he reigned his horse

to a dead stop, leaping from its back to stand in front of Casca.

Grinning, Casca said, "It's good to see you, Jugotai. I had not thought we would meet again before I left. I see you have gained that which you sought."

The boy smiled, dark eyes flashing. He pulled himself up to his full height and stuck out his chest which had started to put some meat on it and no longer resembled a starved chicken breast so strongly.

"Yes, and I have a wife now to bear my sons to fight against the Hsuing-nu."

Casca dismounted and took the boy's hand in the Roman manner of holding the wrists.

"I am pleased and happy for you. You were a good friend and travel companion. I wish you were going with me, but I know that Tsin-ta'i has plans for you here. But, who knows, perhaps we will meet again one day. I must return and if the gods are kind, our paths will cross once more."

The boy's dusky face lit up with pleasure.

"Roman, take the saddle from your mount and put it and your gear on mine. This is my gift to you."

Casca looked from his sleek roan gelding to the runty, shaggy beast that Jugotai wished to trade.

Catching his look, Jugotai laughed. "I am not going to rob you, Roman. This fine animal you ride now will not serve you half as well as this tough nasty-tempered one I wish you to take."

Jugotai thumped the horse on the rib cage listening with a cocked ear to the hollow thump that issued forth.

"This miserable creature was bred and raised in

the mountains and can live on dirt alone for weeks and go without water for days in the desert. He is like us of the Yeuh-chih; perhaps not as pretty as the refined nobles of Rome, but we can go the distance after the fine bloods have dropped over from bad food and water. Believe me, you will not regret the exchange."

The shaggy beast rolled his eyes around and Casca took a good look. The little bastard seemed to be pretty tough.

"Well, Jugotai, if you say he's the horse for me, then so be it."

They swiftly changed saddles and gear. Casca swung himself up into the sheepskin-lined saddle, his feet almost reaching the ground. The nasty-looking horse gave him only one dirty look and ignored him while eating the bark from a tree, even though young grass was easily available.

Jugotai swung into his saddle with the grace of an acrobat and turned the horse's head back to the bridge, whirling his blade above his head. He reared the horse back on his hind legs and cried, "Ride well, Roman. The road is before you. Remember you have friends among the tribes of Kushan. Be not a stranger." With that, Jugotai raced back over the bridge and out of sight.

Days came one on the other as Casca followed the torrents of the Indus through gorges that seemed to drop into the bowels of Hades and rise until he thought it would be possible to touch the stars overhead. Jugotai was right, his cruddy little beast had the agility of a mountain goat and could eat anything, including a portion of one of Casca's tunics he left lying too close to the beast, while he fixed his meal for the day.

Lacking anything better, Casca named the horse Glam, after his old friend at the hold of Helsfjord. There was a resemblance; both were tough and shaggy and had an intelligence that their appearance belied.

Several times Casca met small caravans heading to the lands of the Kushan. From these he would receive information as to the trail ahead. Twice he stopped at what served as an inn for the tough and daring folk of these highlands where he tried as best he could to develop a taste for the fermented mare's milk and curds that the wiry inhabitants smacked their mouths over with such relish. At night they would huddle together in a mass of snoring, foul-smelling bodies. Each would transfer a number of his vermin to those sleeping next to him. Their bed was a large flat stone inside the inn, beneath which a small fire was kept burning to provide warmth. They were a happy folk with great attention paid to manners, almost to the point that it was impossible to talk straight to them.

Weeks passed and Casca finally reached the junction where the Indus was joined by the Panglong Shoa. The two formed a raging muddy torrent where they merged. The great peaks of the Naga Parat were far behind and now the trail passed through ranges that would lead to the desert.

Kicking Glam in the sides with his heels he turned north. Glam never failed him, even when he slept on his back. The horse seemed to have unlimited endurance and would continue on placidly ignoring the man on his back as if he were carrying no more than a feather. In the heights of the

Karakoram pass Casca ate his pack horse and smoked enough of the remaining meat to last him for another week, which should see him through and beyond the Suget.

Finally the Suget side of the pass showed the veins of the mountains, red streaks and bands of granite, massive slabs where the alternating heating and cooling of the mountain-made cracks that finally split and let the boulders break away to leave fresh scars that the winds and time would smooth away in a few centuries.

Four days more and Casca looked out over the basin of the Karim, stretching, it seemed, forever. The descent from his present height of eight thousand feet to the floor below was quick and uneventful. The trail was worn and the thicker air made him almost drunk after his months in the thin air of the Kushan and Indus valleys.

Twelve
THE TARIM

Tsin-ta'i and the map were on the money. The trail leading to the east on the edge of the endless wastes of the Tarim basin was liberally sprinkled with the bones of man and beast; the strangest were the skeletons of the camels, their curved spines looking like huge skeletal snakes with legs.

Examining several of the human remains with a professional eye, Casca found indicators that spoke of violent death; a clean cut in the skull made by a sword, cracked ribs which could have come from a blow with a club or mace and several had arrowheads lodged in the ribs. There was no sign of wooden shafts or anything of wood. As the desert provided little wood, the raiders would naturally have taken any they found usable, even for extra kindling to throw on their fires.

In the three days it took Casca to reach Ho-T'ien, he encountered two caravans, one of which numbered over three hundred pack animals carrying cargoes of rare spices, gems, ivory, slaves and the item most coveted by the matrons of Rome: silk. The caravans were well-armed, escorted by hired bands of mercenaries and slaves who preferred to work for the caravan masters rather than the desert raiders. Many of the mercenaries were Huns remaining from the Eastern tribes that hadn't been forced out by the pressures of the Hsuing-nu and had been migrating in ever greater numbers to the west. These were tough men who had spent so much time in the saddle that their legs were deformed—they could hardly stand on even ground. As children their faces had been seared with red hot irons to stop the growth of beards, leaving only the upper lip with long mustaches that reached below their chins. In contrast, Casca also noticed a number of blue-eyed riders from the Caucasus mountains who were like giants next to the gnome-like Huns when standing. But in the saddle, the Huns with their laminated bows were the equal—if not the master—of all they met.

Casca hoarded his water even though his map showed water only a few days from Ho-T'ien. He felt relief when he reached the banks of the Khotan. He crossed a river shallow enough to be forded and made his way into a prosperous city. The predominant race was the same as Tsin, from Han. These were the merchant princes who bought and sold cargoes for transshipment east and west. Though the largest bulk of commerce went to the west, there was little that the Han needed from the barbarian countries to the west. When the merchants reached their destinations, they would sell all goods, animals and slaves and then wait until enough of them were gathered to hire a new batch of guards to protect them and make the long journey back, this time much faster without the hinderance of pack animals. One successful journey could make a man as rich as a Persian prince. The dangers were great—as attested to by the thousands of bones lying along the trail—but so were the rewards.

Casca made his way through clean streets without the familiar garbage smell of Europe. Bright intelligent faces watched his progress with interest. This was a city that thrived on visitors and anyone unusual might mean money.

Adjusting the small packet that contained the letters from Kushan to the Peacock Throne, Casca swung out of the saddle and handed the reins to a dirty stableboy with eyes much older than his 12 years. Flipping the child a copper coin, he entered the Inn of the Circling Road.

All saloons and taverns have a sameness to them, though the talk may be in different tongues and unfamiliar drinks. Men sat to talk business or politics —Huns, Mongols and Hsuing-nu—all had an unspoken agreement that no blades would be drawn in the city of Ho-T'ien and all arguments would be settled outside the boundaries of the town. Their chieftains knew well the value of the Silk Road, for supplies and weapons could be obtained only with difficulty elsewhere. Though occasionally the city was sacked by a tribe who felt strong enough to get away with it, this had not occurred in ninety years.

The inn was a two-storied building of baked mud, bricks and stone. The inside was lit by the central cooking fire and tallow or oil lamps. Most of the customers had bare arms and chests, or at most, tunics of thin material, their skins and furs put away for the night, which was cold enough to frost a man's breath in these high altitudes with days hot enough to bake a man's brains in his own pan.

The weeks spent in Kushan with Tsin learning what he could of the language of Chin, served him in good stead. Taking a room from the keeper, he spent the next week talking and listening; the melodic tones of the orientals came to him readily. If somewhat stilted in style, he could still make himself understood and each day the feel of the new tongue became a little more natural. He thanked whatever powers there were for his ability to pick up languages. Here also he obtained news of the trail ahead, the best places to water and rest; this information came from the merchants of Chin. The Hsuing-nu, Mongols, and Huns spoke to no one other than their own and, though no blades were drawn, they swaggered through the city like conquerors pushing the milder merchants and visitors out of the way. This was accepted as a fact of life and the people of Ho-T'ien merely sighed and went about their daily business, clucking over the bad manners of the savages.

Rested, Casca decided the time had come for one more leg of his travels. Paying his bill with small coins of silver, he loaded his small horse with skins of water and bought a new pack animal; a wall-eyed bay mare who looked as if she were made out of leather, her legs were good and her teeth showed she still had a few good years left. Though he did not relish eating her, as tough as she looked, he knew he would have to cut off chunks of her and put them under his saddle, riding on them for days until they were tender enough to swallow.

Thumping Glam in the side to get him started, the smaller horse gave one quick snap at Casca's toes to let him know he wasn't pleased to be leaving. The week of good fodder and rest had swelled his belly to the point he looked pregnant.

The morning sun felt good on his face as he rode out. Glam's small hooves kicked up clouds of sand and dust as they rode. Casca settled into the jarring back-aching bounce that horses use when they want to show who's boss. The flat-roofed buildings of Ho-T'ien were not out of sight when the familiar sounds of death reached his ears, wounded horses screaming like women and the lesser deeper battle cries of men in conflict. The sounds even reached the ears of some in the city, but the things that went on outside were none of their concern; the city was all that mattered.

Hesitating for a moment, he started to turn his horse's head around and go back to the city when the sound of a woman's cry was heard. Dropping the pack horse's lead rope, he kicked Glam in the side and galloped forward as he took his shield from his pack. It was round with four steel bosses holding the arm straps inside. He pulled his sword from the scabbard and, leaning over in the saddle, kicked the horse into a run with the wind whipping in his face. The old familiar call to battle began to build along with the pulse racing faster as he crested a small rocky rise.

The scene greeting his eyes was that of a small caravan of about twenty pack animals and thirty men being overwhelmed by a band of Hsuing-nu. Several women were already on the ground, legs spread and being gang raped by the warriors more interested in ass than loot. The remaining men clustered around a fallen camel with a palaquin on its back, the kind in which the women of the rich rode, shielded from the elements. From within, a thin cry of fear reached him from across the distance.

Slapping Glam on the butt with the flat of his sword, he raced, filling his lungs to the bursting point and letting loose a long scream that jerked the heads of the Hsuing-nu around to see what had interrupted their pleasures. The small knot of guards were doing good work holding off the tribesmen, fighting frantically, several sending arrow after arrow into the circling screaming tribesmen, making them keep their distance.

For the most part, the tribesmen were letting them use up their supply of arrows and then it would be all over. Casca leaned over in the saddle and with a long swipe cut through the back of the neck of a Hsuing-nu who was just about to spill his load into the belly of the screaming woman beneath him. The feel of cold steel slicing through the vertebrae kept him from enjoying to the fullest his final moment of sex. Glam trampled two of his comrades under his sharp hooves and whinnied with pleasure.

Casca broke into the circling line of warriors, hacking right and left. The band of Hsuing-nu had no more than fifty when the attack began. The arrows of the defenders had reduced them somewhat, though man-for-man, the guards were no match for the horsemen. Half the guards were dead or dying and the remainder clustered together, several began their death chants.

Casca's short sword stuck in the ribs of a small grease-covered nomad, his blade almost snapping with the force it took to twist and pull it out; then he was finished.

Leaping from the saddle, he quickly bent Glam's right front foreleg under him and threw the horse to his side, next to the sheltering body of a dead camel, then turned to face the Hsuing-nu. Snapping commands to the surviving guards, he whipped them into a line, making them put away their swords, ordering those with spears and lances to stand ready, to place the butts of the spears in the ground and wait.

Facing the enemy and placing his shield on his back to protect it, he ran into the circling line, bending low as he felt the thump of blades striking off his shield. He would swipe and cut the legs out from under any horse that passed within range and then jump back and take another one. The horsemen crowded in, each anxious to kill this stranger and in their own eagerness, they got in each other's way as he leaped in and out among them slashing and striking screaming a strange battle cry: *Odin*. . .

One youngster came too close and Casca leaped and dragged him from his saddle. The boy did not have a full mustache yet or beard and as he kicked and tried to shove his blade into Casca's gut, Casca twisted the boy's wrist bones until they snapped with an audible cracking. He then held the youth in front of him as a shield.

The circling Hsuing-nu halted. The sides of their animals heaving, they stood silent and still. Casca faced the boy first one way and then another, waiting for the attack which did not come. The riders parted and a smaller tribesmen with three heads tied to his saddle pommel, rode between them.

Older than the others with grey thinning hair which hung in greasy wisps down his back, a weathered thick face from years in the sun, he pointed at the boy, crying out in a guttural tongue.

Casca shook his head, to show he couldn't understand. The old man took a breath and shook his head as if trying to find some long unstudied thoughts:

"Mine," he spoke in the tongue of Chin. "Mine." His voice cracked. "Give him, me . . .mine." The youngster squirmed and Casca gave a short jerk that ground the broken bones of the wrist together.

The old man winced at the cry of pain from the boy.

"Give me," the old one extended his hand out pleading.

"The old man's son or grandson and I've got this little shit by the short hairs," thought Casca.

Holding the boy closer to him, Casca pointed to the survivors and back to the city. "They go, I give." He twisted the boy's arm again.

The old man chewed his upper lip, worry written all over him. Pointing his fingers to Casca, he called out, his voice cracking with restrained emotion, "They go. . .you stay." Bobbing his head, he would give so much, but no more and keep face with his men.

"Good enough, you dog thief, but you go to the hills and wait. When they reach the city, I will let this little viper free, but I want enough distance to be able to get a running start before you come after me."

The chieftain bobbed his head in agreement. After all, they were masters of the plains and deserts.

None could outrace them on horseback. Whirling, the Hsuing-nu left in a cloud of sand and dust, riding to the hills Casca had indicated a mile away.

Keeping a close eye on them, Casca made his way back to the cluster of guards where the surviving women who had just been raped lay whimpering.

The guards opened ranks and wondered. Pointing back to the city of Ho-T'ien, Casca ordered, "Get yourselves and the animals that can move out of here. They won't attack until you are inside the city. Before you leave, I would suggest slitting the throats of the wounded men and animals so they will not suffer."

The leader of the guards quickly agreed and sent two of his men to perform the grisly task. The cries of hurt animals and men became less one by one until only the silence of the desert breeze was to be heard.

A man in silken robes carrying a knife that looked out of place, came and bowed low in front of the Roman.

"Oh, noble stranger. I am the merchant Wu ch'ing, whose miserable life you saved. Know also you have protected a gift to his Highness the Emperor Tzin of the Western Kingdom."

With that, he opened the closed curtains of the palaquin and a tiny graceful hand came forth, followed by a face with such beauty it took Casca's breath away.

"This is Li Tsao, Daughter of Light, a gift to the Emperor." The girl of no more than thirteen looked Casca straight in the eyes with no trace of fear, her face perfection, everything in harmony and skin smoother than the finest silk ever woven. Her eyes were like almonds, dark and intelligent, and she moved with a grace unknown to the western world. She took in fully the figure of the man in front of her, the scarred face and hands and hard eyes. He was not unpleasing, if somewhat rough.

Clearing his throat with a sudden feeling of embarrassment, Casca pointed toward the city with his still dripping blade: "You must go now. I don't know how long they will wait."

The girl put her hands up to his sweating face and pulled him down to her. She set her lips on him and pulled the breath from him with the longest sweetest kiss he had ever felt. For the first time she spoke, her voice as delicate and musical as her appearance. "We will meet again, barbarian. Remember me, I am Li Tsao. I am only a gift now, but one day I shall be more."

Casca waited until the last of the caravans and survivors had disappeared over the rise from which he had attacked. Then giving them a few more minutes to be sure, he mounted his horse and holding the young Hsuing-nu warrior by the hair, he placed him where his people could see. Releasing the boy, he kicked Glam in the flanks so hard the ratty little horse farted and took off as fast as his legs could move. Casca accepted the loss of his pack horse stoically. Everytime he helped someone, it seemed to end up costing him one way or another.

The next three days were spent breaking speed records to Keryia and the next city with water a hundred-plus miles away. Jugotai's promise that his gift was tougher and longer-lasting than an ordinary horse proved to be true; the tough animal was indeed a good gift.

Near Keryia, the Hsuing-nu halted the chase, not for reasons of exhaustion but simply that this region belonged to another tribe and even though they and the Hsuing-nu were cousins, they shared little else other than hate for each other, as is common among many families. To enter their hunting grounds would mean war.

Casca was free.

As free as he *could* be.

Exhausted, he walked through the gates of Keryia. He had alternately ridden and run all the way, stopping only when heat and exhaustion threatened to kill his mount. Now two days rest refreshed him and this time he hooked up with a returning merchant who was wealthy enough to afford a large bodyguard of tough wiry men, looking as if they belonged to the same stock as the Hsuing-nu with the name of Hsien-pi.

The journey took three months with stops at the great marshes, past the lesser town of Ch'iehmo, fed by the river of the same name. They marched along the banks of the river to the marshes for two hundred miles, the rivers fed by the great mountains to the south, standing over them like waiting sentinels. On clear days, the ice could be seen clearly though they were hundreds of miles away. From there, near the eastern edge of the marsh, when the sun was in the right position, Casca could see a shimmering to the north about ten miles away. The merchant he had attached himself to said it was a salt basin, known as Lop Nor. From the Lop Nor to Yumen was four hundred miles of barren land, filled only with the howls of desert jackels and the scurrying of lizards.

At Yumen, Casca found a large city of ten or more thousand. Here was the crossroads from east to west and north to south and the southernmost outpost of the Emperor Tzin. It was well garrisoned with tough-looking soldiers standing guard on crenelated mud walls, most of them carrying a weapon he had not seen before. It looked like a miniature arbalest and shot short arrows with tremendous force. A week there told him much and his usage of the language of Chin increased even more. Minding his own business, he watched everything and was watched, though with courtesy. He was asked his business by a plain looking man with an air of importance and when shown the packet of letters from the King of Kushan, was bothered no more. Messengers were favored and not to be interfered with in the business of kings.

Glam grew fat again in a short time. His powers of recuperation were almost as outstanding as Casca's. The road to the Jade Gate was clear and well marked. When he left Yumen behind, he knew he was on the final part of his journey. The name itself had a magic to it—The Jade Gate—or was it that he still sometimes in his sleep felt on his face the mask of Jade he once wore among the Teotec tribes so far away?

A steady gait dissolved the miles behind him. He was now heading southwest, keeping the Na Shan mountains to the right. He traveled on; summer was full on them and usually he rode at night, taking shelter in the shade of crags and crevices until the worst of the heat was done. He would ride on, lost in his thoughts and dreams of his life and past and what might be, while sitting on Glam's back, like a hairy ship. He dozed and dreamed of faces and sounds which rocked him on his journey: Rome, Persia, Germania, the hold at Helsfjord, the Roman square standing with locked shields or forming the tortoise to assault a city's walls. And always he awoke with the sour taste of battle in his mouth.

Thirteen
THE WALL

One-thousand-five-hundred miles of stone forming the greatest single work in the life of the world, turned and twisted, like a monstrous serpent, and seemed to fall back on itself as it crested the twisting mountains and turned and finally disappeared over the horizon.

Casca wore a cloak of wild goatskin and breeches of camelskins made pliable by the chewing of the hides and scraping and pounding of the women of the Yueh-chih.

The wind was blowing from behind, in from the plains. Soon the direction would change and the wind come from the seas bringing the spring rains and floods, but for now the jacket and breeches were welcome to cut the chill edges that searched through the lacings of his clothes. His hair had grown long and hung to his shoulders; his face was darkened by the winds and the sun.

Old Shao Tze was right, the wall seemed to run forever. He had told Casca on the galley that it had been started by the Emperor Shih Huang Ti, two hundred and fourteen years before the birth of the crucified prophet, Yesuah. It had been designed to keep out the marauding Mongolian peoples who preceded the Huns.

Riding alongside the wall, after four days he finally came to a portal where one of the permanent garrisons was maintained. Frequently he had seen mounted riders and archers watching him from the walls, but no words were spoken. However, long before he reached the portal, his coming was well known.

From the height of the wall, he resembled to the watchers one of the wandering nomads of the steppes. Stopping for the night in the sheltered crevices among the rocks, he would feed on chunks of horsemeat which he placed under his saddle and rode on to tenderize it; learning from the nomads, he made use of the droppings of horsemen long since gone, to build his small campfires and keep the worst of the chill away until he rolled up in his blanket of felt and slept until the break of each dawn, which would bring a greater chill stirring him to waking. He would eat cold horsemeat, washed down with a draft of strong-tasting water from the goatskin sacks that served as canteens and ride on. Often he would have to stop and lead his shaggy-haired horse over the rougher spots, marveling at how the little beast could eat almost anything and still keep its strength. The finest steeds from the imperial stables of Rome would have starved to death in the first week if they had to subsist on the same diet of some of the wild beasts of the high plains of Asia.

Standing before the portal, he called out in the language of Chin. It was close enough so many of the watchers could make out what he was saying: "I bear a message for the King of Tzin from the Tribes of the Yueh." Holding a scroll above his head to the watchers on the towers, he hoped this might lend emphasis to his words.

The great gates swung open on iron hinges which were kept oiled to keep the rust away and squeaking under the strain of their massive weight. They opened and Casca was told to enter with a wave of a lance.

Entering a courtyard, he was greeted by a contingent of armed pikemen and archers carrying the strange curved bows of laminated horn and sinew that could drive an arrow four hundred yards with killing efficiency and could wound at eight hundred. The bowmen wore wrist guards of wood and ivory to protect their gut strings. Silently they stood in the ranks, orderly and disciplined, watching through dark intelligent eyes.

Casca was brought to the commander, Sung Ti Aman. Taller than his subordinates, he looked with distaste at the barbarian before him, wrinkling his nose at the high odor that came his way from this rider.

Nevertheless, he performed the prescribed rules of etiquette required to be given to any messenger from a chieftain of another tribe.

Casca took his place downwind from Sung Ti Aman who, after making the usual courteous inquiries, requested to see the scroll bearing the words of the Chief of the Yueh-chih.

The scroll had been written by a learned man living with the tribe who had left the realms of the Chin because of legal problems. The calligraphy was properly done and sophisticated enough in style that it gave the words written a degree of worth.

Food was brought, brown rice and vegetables artistically arranged to please both the eye and the palate; delicate morsels of river fish on bamboo spears in thin sauces tasted like paper to Casca after his long diet of raw meat and millet, but it was more filling than it appeared, the rice settling comfortably in his gut.

The commander made a gift to Casca of a clean tunic and trousers; anything to get rid of the odor of the damp sheepskin.

Sung Ti perused the contents of the scroll, pondering how best they could be transported to the court of the Son of Heaven. The regular courier service was not due for another fortnight and he was too short manned to send any of his men the long way. The next imperial courier station was two hundred miles to the south.

Casca was shown to the quarters kept for guests and basins of water were brought to him, to clean himself if he was so inclined. He was. After washing, his face felt like the ass of a newborn babe, lighter in color from the wind-burned cheeks and brow. Putting on a tunic of plain silk and trousers of loose wool tucked into his boot tops, he entered the compound.

Taking in the appearance and equipment of his

host's soldiers, he noted most wore jazerins of scaled armor and helmets of lacquered wood, embossed with ornamental plaques of brass and bronze. Everything clean and in its place, the men were well-ordered and mannerly, no sign of rowdiness. They looked to be quite efficient, though, to his way of thinking, their armor would scarcely stand up to the heavier blades of the Roman or Germanic tribes. The bowmen impressed him the most. Several were having target practice in the courtyard, sending arrow after arrow unerringly into the target set some two hundred paces away, the arrows sinking half their length into the fiber targets, attesting to the power of the bow.

Sung Ti sent for him and was more impressed with his strange guest now that he was clean. The strength of the visitor from beyond his world was evident in the twisted cords of his forearms and the way his eyes never missed anything. Sung Ti knew his guest was a warrior to be reckoned with, but, more important, for a barbarian he had a remarkable set of manners. And though he made several errors in etiquette, he, after all, had not had the training in the graces of civilized society. Sung Ti had never seen eyes like Casca's. To him they resembled some of the high lakes.

It was well known the Emperor had a great curiosity for the strange and unusual. Feeling his problem solved, Sung Ti decided Casca would be his messenger to the court with a letter from him. Casca should have no trouble traveling the three hundred miles to the Court of Tzin where the Emperor was now in spring residence.

That night, the two found many common interests, especially after several cups of the wet looking milky wine Sung Ti poured into lacquered cups. Soldiers, like physicians, will always find something of mutual interest to talk and argue over.

Casca showed him his Gladius Iberius. The short blade and thickness of the steel was odd to the eyes of his host, but after his guest had done him the honor of showing him his weapon, Sung Ti could do no less.

Taking his blade from its engraved scabbard of rare woods, he drew it in the proper manner and set it on a cushion in front of Casca. The handling of the blade by its master told Casca that he was observing a ceremony of great meaning and was being honored. Sung Ti laid a silk scarf beside the cushion and sat back on his heels waiting for the foreigner's response.

Casca, watching his host carefully, bowed and indicated the weapon and scarf, careful to touch neither. Sung Ti smiled and nodded in the affirmative, pleased his barbarian with lake eyes had the good grace to show courtesy. Taking the scarf, Casca was careful not to touch the blade with his hands. He held it lengthwise in front of him and examined it slowly from hilt to point, making quiet sounds of approval. The blade was long and slightly curved, the edge on one side only, coming to a tapered point designed for slashing, not stabbing, though it could be used for that purpose. The weapon told him a great deal about the fighting techniques of the owner. The stylized manner of presenting the weapon for his inspection said that here was an honored and rigid warrior class.

Clucking his tongue in approval, he bowed low

and placed the piece on the cushion exactly as it had been presented, careful to be slow and deliberate in his handling and again not to touch the blade.

Sung Ti hissed between his teeth in approval and once again presented the blade, this time with his own hands that his guest might feel the quality of the steel.

Casca knew by this act that he had done well and gained merit in the eyes of the commander of the garrison and was being accepted not only as an emissary but as an equal. Carefully and gently, as if touching a woman, he ran his fingers over the blade, feeling the satin sheen of fine steel. The grain of steel was as fine as the silk robes his host wore. The fine edge gave it a new importance in his eyes. The grace with which the sword was handled and ceremoniously wiped clean, then returned to its scabbard increased his respect. This was a cultured and dangerous people to whom form and manners were weapons, and offense would be easily taken at any affront to their honor.

Casca thanked his host for the honor shown him: "Commander," he bowed again, "forgive me if I do not have the words or proper training of your people to show the depths of my gratitude for the honor you have shown me. Indeed, beside the glory of your weapon, mine is but a poor tool, fit only for common usage. If I make errors in your customs, please forgive me as this is not intentional. I am only an ignorant soldier, who has not the advantages of your great culture."

Sung Ti smiled openly for the first time and clapped Casca on the shoulder with a friendly hand.

"The words of the sage say that the way to enlightenment is to know one's ignorance. Once that is clear, he may learn and advance. To be ignorant is no crime. To refuse to be otherwise is an insult. You are welcome and shall take the treaty of Yueh-chih to the Son of Heaven with your own hands. Now, let us talk of things we both know and appreciate. Let us tell of our battles and loves. I am curious—is it true that many of the women of your lands have the same blue eyes and hair like grain in the sun?"

Fourteen
LAND OF TZIN

Sung Ti offered Casca the use of one of the horses of his stables but the offer was graciously refused. Casca had grown fond of the tough shaggy horse that had carried him so far. He did accept, with gratitude, the present of a short dagger—a miniature of the sword Sung Ti had shown him. Sung Ti had informed the blade was quite old and was a little son to his own blade, made by the same master craftsman over a hundred years ago and had rested by the father blade for that time, but now was perhaps the time for the son to leave home and serve a new master, even perhaps grow into a full sword. Sung Ti's smooth face and dark eyes twinkled at his joke as he bade farewell to the stranger.

Riding a well paved road, the miles slipped behind as Casca entered the lands of Tzin.

Passing through more populated villages, the seal given him by Sung Ti proclaiming him an imperial messenger sped his movement rapidly. Everywhere the seal was honored and food and shelter given without question, though he did receive questioning stares from the people. At one village he had his hair trimmed back to the nape of his neck and had a hard time talking the barber out of shaving the hair on the sides, leaving only a mane that would tie in the back, a style that was becoming popular among the young warrior nobility. The reason for the mane was to give their enemies something to hang to if their heads were taken as trophies. Casca had no intention of losing his head and passed up the offer to make him more stylish, much to the barber's disappointment.

Many of the cities he passed through as he neared the home of the Emperor were walled with moats and strange-looking tiered structures. Straight lines and gently curving angles, sloping tiled roofs and temples, like the food, were designed to be in harmony with the land and surroundings, but built to last. Casca knew the structures to be solid, having built not a few fortifications during his years in the Legion and, although no engineer, he could see strength in the design.

As he came closer to the heartland, the land became more cultivated and caravans of merchants poured into the urban centers, bringing their loads on the back of two-humped camels and asses, horses and ox carts, loaded with those things which make a nation live.

Several times he was confronted by warriors on horseback, proud men in rich trappings of silk and gold, marvelous patterns of delicate scenes of the countryside and graceful flowers woven in threads of fine gold and silk, seeming not to be out of place on these warriors of the Tzin. Here art and war seemed to be in perfect blending. The courage of the warriors was clear and their affection for delicate and beautiful things did nothing to lessen their masculinity; indeed, it often served to accent the subtle danger that would come if one of these Asian equestrians was offended.

Fifteen
CH'ANG-AN

Casca entered the walls of the city Ch'ang-an after careful scrutiny by the officer in charge on the moongate entrance. After inspection of the seals on the letters from the King of Kushan and Commander of the Jade Gate, he provided an escort that led the foreigner through the streets of the city to the quarters where the emissaries of foreign courts were provided the hospitality of the Tzin Emperor until such time as the Son of Heaven could see them.

The escort was friendly and curious. Never had he seen anyone like this big man on the wiry mountain pony. The city of Tzin was well laid out with wide streets formed into walled blocks. There were over three hundred and fifty of these, each walled enclosure a smaller city unto itself with gates that closed at sundown. There being no traffic between the smaller cities, there was less chance for riot or revolt.

Inside, the wards were only narrow paths that had to be traveled on foot. Even the most noble visitor would have to dismount and enter on foot. The buck-toothed smiling guide informed Casca that Ch'ang-an was like all the other cities of the Emperor, laid out with the royal palace facing south so that all who approached would come from the north. To face south was a sign of superiority, none could have more than the Son of Heaven. Of course, there were rare occasions when the Emperor would, as a sign of respect or favor, greet a great man or loyal subject on an east or west line, but this was rare indeed and only happened twice that the guide could remember.

Entering a ward with walls forty feet high and sentries on guard, they passed through a rounded gate with bars that could lower instantly, leaving holes from which archers could fire. The tiled roofs and gardens within were laid out in a manner strange to his eyes. Placement of such common objects as a few odd-shaped rocks set on raked gravel gave an oddly comforting effect, even peaceful. Fragile as the small gardens appeared, they looked as if they would endure forever, captured in a moment of time, preserved for the ages.

His smiling host showed him to three rooms in which were graceful ink drawings and strange airy paintings, of almost ethereal quality. His guide bowed on leaving, saying others would come soon to see to his needs.

There were no chairs in the room. Casca sat on a large cushion to take his boots off, wincing at the odor. He had been told his horse was in the imperial stables and his gear would be brought to him later. The absence of his sword bothered him, but he had been left with the small belt dagger of Sung Ti as a sign of trust. Leaning back, his eyes blinked once and then closed.

He was awakened by the rustling of silk robes. As his eyes snapped open, a gentle face appeared in focus, eyes like those of a mountain doe, hair piled high on her head, held by combs of jade and ivory set with long pins, jeweled with sapphires on the tips.

The girl smiled shyly as she too looked at the barbarian from beyond the edge of the world. Hesitantly, she motioned for him to follow her.

Leading him with graceful tiny steps, she took him through a series of paneled and paper-walled rooms to a tiled bath of lapis lazuli, indicating for him to enter the water. As she helped him remove his clothing she looked at him curiously, then motioned for him to enter the steaming water.

Sighing deeply, Casca lowered himself into the water to his chest. After the long months on the trail the hot water was ecstasy. The girl rolled up her long sleeves and began to wash his back with perfumed oils and soap. She was soon joined by three others, each as beautiful and curious. Among them they left, to Casca's delight, no part of his body unscrubbed.

Rising from the bath, he was given clean fresh robes with emblems in ideograms he could not understand, but which obviously provided him an identity for whatever status he had in this palace of delights.

The girls chattered merrily among themselves, comparing his anatomy and exclaiming over the wealth of scar tissue that crisscrossed his body. The deep scar on his chest seemed to fascinate them almost as much as the hair on his chest, which they had competed for the right to wash and giggled at the feel while wondering among themselves what it would feel like next to their own skin, for the men of their race had no such thing. Even if the big nose was ugly, he was somehow not unappealing.

The girl who had first come for him almost fell over when Casca asked her in her own language if she would like to find out how the hair on his chest would feel next to her own smooth bosom. Giggling, she hid her face behind one long silk sleeve and beckoned for him to follow her again, this time returning him to his rooms where he found all his gear was gone and even more clothes awaiting his approval.

For the first time, the girl spoke directly to him, her voice like one of the melodic wind chimes he had seen hanging from the tree branches in the courtyard: "Food will be brought soon, barbarian. Your clothes are being burned. They are not fit for this place. You are being shown the honors and courtesies required by law to be given to an imperial messenger from another king—no more and no less. I am Mei Cho, a slave, and perhaps I will be permitted to serve you while you are in residence in this garden."

Giggling she stammered, "You really are so very ugly. . ."

Laughing still, she fled outside and disappeared down a tiled walkway.

Three days Casca waited, growing ever more restless but still not permitted to leave the confines of the garden. At night he watched the rocks and sand; they seemed to want to tell him something, if only he could see. Twice men of the court had come and questioned him politely as to what he had encountered on the trail of the silk road, making notes on what looked like papyrus, writing with long graceful strokes.

On the third night, while sitting on the bench placed so that one could view the garden, he sat watching the light from the moon cast shadows over the garden, lighting one place and casting another into darkness. A shadow crossed him. Standing, he turned around to see a young man wearing only a simple robe of gray linen watching him.

The young man bowed and moved closer, "Forgive me, honored sir, if I have disturbed your moment."

Casca bowed likewise. The moon lit up the youngster's face, smooth in the light. His eyes were gentle yet wiser than his years.

Casca indicated the carved stone bench. "Will you join me, young master? The night is quiet and there is room for more than one. I would be honored for you to share your company with me." Damn, he thought to himself, I am beginning to talk like them, it must be contagious.

The youngster moved with smooth strong steps to the bench, sat down and folded his hands, one on the other. Both were silent for a moment and then the boy pointed to the garden with long graceful fingers. "For what do you look in the garden, Lord Casca?"

"I don't know, young sir, but it draws me. I believe the stones and gravel have a special meaning."

The boy nodded. "Indeed, that is why it is what it is. One of the greatest poets of our land built this small piece of perfection over two hundred years ago. It is his message and feelings that draw you."

"Yes," agreed Casca. "I never thought of it before, but it is like a poem, if only I could understand the words."

The boy smiled showing even white teeth. "Perhaps you will before this night is out. Watch the garden and I will try to help you."

Casca let his eyes drift over the shadows and sands settling on one lone rock sitting by itself apart from the others and somehow seeming like him, part of the whole, but always alone. The boy's voice merged with the garden. "Yes, it is alone, that one common rock is humanity, placed by itself, as it has been for two hundred years. It was put there for all who are lonely to see and know they are not the only ones who must be lonely and even the most humble of objects has feeling too." Pointing to where the two larger stones were connected by a piece of weathered rope, tying the larger stone to the smaller, he continued, "That is man and woman when Chu Ssma placed them there. He took pity on them in their isolation and made them one by giving the thread of life to connect them, to give them comfort though there is a distance between them. Now they are happy and have each other. They shall be so as long as this place exists."

Though the concepts were alien to the Roman, they seemed here not out of place. Watching the two rocks with their tattered rope, it made sense to him and was oddly pleasing and comforting.

The two sat silently until the first light of day cast a glow over the wall. Rising, the young man bowed low to the barbarian, "We will meet again, Lord Casca," and he turned to leave.

"Please, young sir, you know my name, may I ask yours? I wish to thank you properly for what you have shown me tonight."

The young man smiled again and bowed gently, "I am Tzin."

Before Casca could find his voice, he was gone.

"The Emperor. . .I have spent a whole night with the Emperor watching a couple of rocks!"

Confused, he returned to his rooms and lay on his pallet, letting sleep take him. "The Emperor. . ."

That day he dreamed again, faces haunting him. . .Glam. . .the barbarian. . .Neta, his first love. . .ships and battles and then a distant aching in his wrist and the Elder Dacort's face leering from a cross saying. . .'You are the road that leads to Jesus and we shall be there with you.'

The following day, Casca was instructed in the manner in which to present himself to the Emperor. He would enter the imperial chambers on his knees and bow three times, crawl forward three paces and bow three more times, keeping his eyes averted from the Son of Heaven until he was permitted to sit up, but not to stand as no one must hover over the royal person.

The reception hall of the Peacock Throne was quite simple in comparison to the courts of Rome and other kingdoms he had seen. Ostentation was not to be found here. Wealth, yes, in the few objects present, but the lack of any vulgar display seemed somehow to give those items present an even greater value. Vases of alabaster so thin that light glowed from them as if there were candles inside, one statuette of a flying dove carved of luminescent rose jade placed on a piece of twisted teak, spoke more of wealth and power than all the jewels on the fingers of Gaius Nero.

Performing the prescribed ritual, Casca bowed his way into the presence of the royal person. His face remained to the mat floor until the words of the major-domo permitted him to rise and look upon the face of the Father of the World, conqueror of the Hsuing-nu, overlord of the mongol tribes and the Son of Heaven, in whom all wisdom resides.

Tzin sat in the only chair present, on a raised dais so that even sitting, he would be taller than any man present. In his hands, he held a wand of gold and ivory, beautifully engraved with twisting four-toed dragons winding about it. Four toes on a dragon were permitted only for those of the royal household and only they were permitted to carry them or their likenesses about.

A small brazier glowed nearby the Emperor's right hand, a thin spiral of incense rising and giving the delicate fragrance of roses. The Emperor had more wealth on him than the treasuries of Rome could purchase in three years of taxes from all provinces, but it was considered vulgar to complement each other in this place. On his head was a soft two-cornered cap with red and gold tassels, his robes and hat were both of the imperial green shade that only nobility could wear.

The Emperor spoke, holding the packet of letters

which Casca had brought from Kushan. "Lord Casca, we thank you for bringing us this welcome message from his highness, the King of Kushan. We are pleased to note that our countryman, Tsin-ta'i, still has our interests at heart and is loyal to the throne. Kushan has prospered and an alliance to drive the Hsuing-nu back into the wastes from which they came, shall please us."

Holding up another letter, the Emperor continued, "Here is a letter from our servant, Tsin-ta'i, in which he tells the remarkable story set down by an ancient sage who died long ago, Shin Lao Tze. It is indeed remarkable. None other than myself has seen this letter." Tzin dropped the paper onto the incense brazier where the flames hungrily consumed the paper, leaving only a small pile of ashes.

"Lord Casca, is it your wish to remain with us and serve the House of Tzin for such time as you wish to depart, as I know you must one day?"

Casca looked the young king in the eyes and felt again the drawing power of this young man. "It is, Lord."

Pleased, Tzin nodded and motioned for a scribe to crawl nearer. "Take these words. It is my pleasure that the one known as Casca shall henceforth be honored as the Baron of Chung Wei, which guards the Jade Gate from which he came to us. There all shall obey and honor him." Pointing his ivory rod, the Emperor said, "Lord Casca, you shall await my pleasure and prepare the men I shall send to do battle against the Hsuing-nu. From our mutual friend in Kushan, I know much of you and that you will be of assistance in ridding the earth of the lice who call themselves men." Tzin clapped his hands and had a lacquered box brought to him. Opening the container, he withdrew the new lord's seal, presenting it to Casca with his own hands. The *Chu hou wang* of a noble, made of yellow gold with a knob of polished tortoise shell. With this Casca would make his mark, sign his orders and all documents sent to the Lord of Heaven. The Lord Tzin himself signed and stamped documents of ennoblement with his own hand and the seal of the kingdom made of rare jade engraved with a *li*, a one-horned dragon knob with four toes bearing the inscription that had come down to the Kings of Han from the past: *Shou t'ien chih ming huang ti shou ch'ang* (By the command of heaven, long-lived and glorious the emperor).

Honor was shown to the new lord, responsibility was given and none could dispute it. The word of the Emperor was law and the law would be obeyed, for such is the order of things in civilized countries.

"You have my permission to go to your province now," said the Emperor and, with the wave of his sceptor, informed Casca that the audience was over. Repeating the same procedure used on entering, Casca backed out, averting his eyes from the Presence and not rising until the chamber doors closed behind him.

"A Baron! He's made me a Baron of Tzin. Well, why not, I was a god once."

Sixteen
BARON OF CHUNG WEI

Casca left the Capitol a noble with a retinue of men-at-arms and knights, along with servants and carts to carry his possessions—enough to outfit a Persian palace. He departed riding a bay stallion with white stocking, a brave flash on his forehead. He cut a dashing figure on the beautiful and high spirited animal and the brass rings which held his feet made the ride much easier. Casca stared at the brass rings thinking, "Why didn't we ever think of them? These people have had them for centuries and can make the most ungainly foot soldier into a horseman. Shit, it took me years to learn how to ride without them and not fall off every time that damned horse shied at a bush or snake."

Behind, faithful, tough old Glam was being led on a tether by a slave. Casca looked at him fondly. "If there is fighting in the deserts and hills, I would rather have him than ten of these thin-blooded race horses."

Behind shaggy Glam came Mei Cho giggling to

herself as she recalled how the hair on the ugly one's chest had felt the first time. But he was naive. She was his first girl and as such had seniority over any others he might take. She lounged in her palanquin stretched between horses and thought how she would make life miserable for the other girls if they didn't jump at her commands. Her only regret about her appearance was that her feet were too large. She had been born to slaves and was unlucky enough not to have had them bound as a baby, for the tiny feet that came with binding made them slow when it came to following orders, but the big nosed one didn't even seem to notice. "He is really kind not to hurt my feelings by commenting on how ugly my feet are."

The way back was pleasant and the weather cool. Winter was not far off and the leaves were just turning gold and red, setting the hills on fire with color. Twice he had the pleasure of running into some of the same bravados he had met going to the capitol and thoroughly enjoyed making them perform Kowtow as he now outranked them by some distance. Through winding valleys and rivers they rode, taking their time and enjoying the countryside, watching the villagers on their daily business. "How could they allow their feet to be mutilated?" he mused, thankful Mei didn't have such a deformity. The girls who worked at the factories had to be brought in on wheelbarrows, riding in baskets on the side to do their work and returned to their homes in the same manner.

Boundary stones marked the limits of each province and, after a month, a rider came to him to tell him the borders of Chung Wei were just over the next rise. Spurring his horse in the flanks, he raced ahead with his bodyguard and stopped at the stone marker. Over a thousand villagers were prostrated on their faces waiting for him to cross. They had come to see their new lord and make him welcome. Dismounting, he stepped across the boundary.

Calling out and talking to the backs presented, he called loudly, "I am your lord. Serve me well and I will serve you likewise. If you have complaints, I will find you justice. If you are dishonest, I will punish you. Be loyal to your Emperor and to me. Follow his commands and we will get along. Now, rise and face me as men should."

The villagers rose to their feet at his command, watching as Casca mounted his horse and rode among them, following the trail to the castle. Village leaders and elders came forward and made gifts of pigs and grain while gongs were beaten to frighten off evil spirits that might try to bring bad fortune to this day and their new master. He was strange looking enough to them without having a curse put on him by a jealous ghost. They had not had a real master for some time now and only the tax collectors came at the end of each harvest to collect the Emperor's tithe. They were a glad people now. Without a master they felt incomplete. There was no one to give them justice or tell them what to do.

The deserted castle of Chung Wei held enough rooms for a thousand warriors and a hundred horses. Dust covered everything but nothing had been removed. All had been left as it was when the previous master had been sent to join his ancestors for trying to incite rebellion and make alliance with the Hsuing-nu.

Mei Cho gave everyone hell, shouting orders and

threatening the most vile of punishments until in a remarkably short time, the castle was restored to a decent condition, making maximum use of the new furniture and paintings she had so carefully packed before leaving the capitol. This was her home now and would look like one.

Casca's first act was to send for the commander of the garrison at the Jade Gate. Next he set about organizing his forces and familiarizing himself with their weapons and tactics. The most amazing finding was their use of the crossbow, those miniature arbalests; five bolts could be set in a wooden slot on top and fired as fast as the operator could recock with the lever provided for such a purpose. A powerful and most efficient weapon. Like the Hsuing-nu and the Huns, they relied heavily on mounted archers for the mobile units and placed men with long spears to the front to ward off enemy cavalry while crossbow men behind them would pick them off with their bolts, swordsmen and auxiliaries filled the rest of the ranks. But their structure was too rigid and not given to making use of maximum mobility in turning to face an enemy who attacked from the oblique or flank position. "Well," thought Casca, "a few weeks of good Roman short order drill would take care of that."

In the stables he found a number of stout-looking chariots that had been there for an unknown period of time, but in good repair. An idea began to creep around the edges of his mind. "True, by today's modern standards, chariots had long since become outmoded for warfare against individual mounted units, but still, they might be useful. . ."

Casca ordered the chariots refurbished and the wheels greased so they could be used instantly if needed. He also had a strong loop of brass tied to each side of the chariots and connected under the floorboards by a strong brass band, the purpose for which he kept to himself.

Sung Ti presented himself in a flash, racing into the courtyard with a small escort. He swung down from the saddle and strode to the great room where audiences were held. Casca rose at his entrance and spoke to him: "Get up, Sung Ti. You are my first friend in the land of Chin and I welcome you as such. You have my permission to enter my presence and not perform Kowtow. You're a man, stand like one and as an equal. You are welcome. Now, come and sit with me. We have much of which to speak."

Casca dismissed those present and he and Sung Ti were left alone together except for Mei Cho who stayed to serve her man and his friend, though with a slight sense of displeasure at the honor the Baron had shown this common soldier.

"Bring me up to date on what's happening on the frontier, Sung Ti. And what may I do to help you?"

Sung Ti eyed Casca's woman. "A pretty thing, even if she does have ugly feet," he thought. Turning to Casca, he spoke, "My lord, the Hsuing-nu are becoming bolder. It has been too long since last they were taught a lesson and their numbers increase with each year. They are like desert fish which lay eggs by the thousand and each year there are more. As of late, they have been attacking caravans with impunity and taxing those they choose to let pass."

Casca thought a moment and then spoke, "Has a messenger from his Highness gone through the Jade Gate to Kushan?"

"Yes, several have gone through, all with strong escorts and well mounted. At least one should make it. Can you tell what is happening?"

Casca laid out the Emperor's orders. Depending on the response which came back from Kushan next spring, they could mount a combined offensive against the Hsuing-nu. The general plan was for the armies of Tzin to ride wide across the desert and come in from behind the barbarians, thus forcing them to the mountains where the Kushan forces would ambush them in the passes and hold them until Tzin army could come up and, between the two, could eliminate these human vermin once and for all.

Sung Ti fairly glowed with pleasure. "Good, it has been too long." Then, with a touch of anxiety, "You will take me with you, my lord?"

Casca clapped him on the shoulder. "Yes, I want to see how you use that long blade of yours. In Han, I have seen no other like it. They all have conventional looking swords with straight edges and points. I want to see how your weapon compares. If it's good, we might make it standard issue for my men."

"By the way, has a caravan come through with a young girl named Li Tsao? She is being sent to the Emperor as a gift. I met her and her escort on the trail here some months back, and was just wondering if they made it through."

Sung Ti shook his head. "I would know if they had come through the Jade Gate, but as I said, the savages have been killing and plundering with impunity and who knows, she may now be servicing a barbarian or may yet be in one of the cities on the edge of the Silk Road, waiting until it is safe to pass. One does not take chances with the Emperor's property."

Seventeen
THE WAR LORD

Two seasons passed for Casca in his mountain stronghold. The castle resembled the more familiar structures of Rome and the Empire; square and solid, with sharp angles and parapets, it had been built for the security of the Emperor Shih Huang Ti, whose workers built this section of wall six hundred years ago. It was as solid now as when the first stones were joined.

Sung Ti had long since returned to his post and visited on several occasions to let Casca know the Emperor's gift had come safely through and the girl Li Tsao was now in residence in the capitol. Casca wondered how she fared with the young Emperor.

Imperial messengers and inspectors visited to see how the new Baron was faring and if he was administering his domain properly. They returned with good reports of the state and readiness of the army he had gathered and trained. His habit of listening personally to the complaints of his peasants gave him an ear to the people.

The emperor sent word that in the spring they would march against the Hsuing-nu. Messengers had come and gone between the Han and Kushan Empire. Between them, they would smash the Hsuing-nu once and for all. In the spring when the snows melted and the high passes were clear, the armies of Kushan would march while the forces of Tzin followed on the Silk Road. They would crush the Hsuing-nu between them in the passes of the high plateaus.

Casca's admiration for the stamina and intelligence of his subjects knew no bounds. They were absolutely loyal and would follow orders to the letter, even when they found them strange. Most confusing was their lord's refurbishing and ordering of new chariots to be built. They had long since been an obsolete weapon, but still the carpenters toiled to produce even more of them and the blacksmiths made long chains of iron—for what purpose they could not fathom. They had learned that their round-eyed master had a reason for all he did and that was enough. They would know in good time what lay in the mind of their scarred lord.

With the swelling of the streams and rivers from the first thaw, messengers rode to the castle with the word that the Son of Heaven approached with a great army and that Casca should make ready to march. Stores were readied for transport and caches of food were sent by advance parties far ahead to be used on the trail where there would be little to feed an army of the magnitude that would soon be riding over the dry wastes of the deserts. Sixty thousand warriors and cavalry, the cream of the empire were already near the Jade Gate. Casca would join them there in seven days.

Casca's five thousand soldiers and two hundred chariots left their land behind. The women wailed and children tugged at their fathers' sleeves. All knew many would not return. Like the mystical serpent, the army marched through winding valleys and canyons. Cavalry in front and in scouting positions followed by the chariots, each carrying its load of chains behind came the slower infantry with a cavalry escort covering the rear of the column.

Dark was upon them when they reached the Jade Gate. The lights of the cooking fires below them lit the valley like a million fireflies, stretching for miles. Leaving his forces to bivouac on high ground, Casca first washed and clothed himself in fresh robes of sky blue silk and went to pay his homage to his liege lord, Tzin.

Presenting himself to the imperial steward, he was announced and admitted to the Presence. Entering as required, he performed Kowtow and was given permission to rise and make his report to the emperor.

The two years had filled the youngster out, his shoulders were wider and there was a trace of a beginning beard, but his eyes still sparkled with the good humor and brilliance of youth. Several general officers and councilors stood silently, gorgeous in the royal uniforms and armor of red and black. A reclining figure on a divan to the left and rear of the Emperor made him catch his breath as he had on the desert. Li Tsao. More beautiful than he remembered, more of a woman now with promise of even greater beauty to come.

"I was right. The little bitch has done well by herself to be permitted to travel with the Emperor and be present at a meeting of the general staff."

Li Tsao smiled at him and covered her mouth with an ivory fan painted with love scenes.

Clapping his hands, tables were brought to the Emperor and set in front of him forming a half circle on which were placed maps showing the regions they would be fighting and crossing. Using the map as a reference, the Emperor's generals outlined their plan. In the valleys between Changyeh and Chini-a, they would trap the Hsuing-nu between the armies of the Empire and that of the Kushan, but they needed something that would make the Hsuing-nu gather at the proper moment. Hsuing-nu prisoners and slaves had been permitted to escape after first working on a great treasure of jewels and gold, enough to make the most wary barbarian throw caution to the wind, enough to buy an empire in the west if they chose. The escaped slaves reported to their chieftains that it was the wedding gift to the Emperor from the King of Kushan and that he was to take a daughter of the Kushan king as his Empress. Ten thousand warriors were to take the treasure to Kushan and return with the Emperor's bride. This had also been confirmed by spies in Kushan. The Hsuing-nu were determined to have the treasure for themselves and ten thousand imperial warriors meant they would have to call all the tribes together to insure victory. They had faced the disciplined warriors of Tzin before. Even now a hundred thousand barbarians were gathering in great conclaves at the oasis and marshes along the route of march that the treasure must be brought. The ten thousand were already two days ahead on the trail in the valley of Changyeh. They would halt and once again escaping slaves would take a message to their chieftains that the royal emissary had become too ill to be moved. Physicians were in constant attendance to him, a cousin of the Emperor. The treasure party would remain where they were until he was well enough to travel and from the talk of the physicians around the campfires, it appeared he would be ill for some time, perhaps even weeks.

Hearing this news, the Hsuing-nu council of chieftains decided to move. Controlling the wild warriors was difficult at any time but to sit idle for an unknown period of time was impossible. Besides, if they struck now, numbers would be on their side and they would be able to strike and get away before any reinforcements could be sent. True, they would have the garrison of Yumen behind them but they were of a few numbers and little consequence. The treasure waited for them.

The tribes gathered in the thousands, riding in several long columns miles apart like a line of ants, crossing the deserts and plains, converging on the valley.

"Sly bastards," mused Casca, "these yellow men certainly don't suffer from a lack of deviousness. It's a good plan and the army of Kushan is already on the march now that the Hsuing-nu have withdrawn their tribes from their borders for this great raid."

The Hsuing-nu had no fear of the Kushan; never had their forces left their boundaries in pursuit of them. The Kushan were content to remain at home and if a fight was necessary, they would do it there. Kushan, they knew would be no threat.

Tzin questioned Casca as to his need for the two hundred chariots he had bought. Of what use could they be against the more agile and faster cavalry of the savages. The horsemen would merely ride around them and shoot them down from the rear. The Roman begged permission to explain and the Emperor then broke into pleased and delighted chuckles once he heard the Baron's plan. Nodding among themselves, the generals agreed that perhaps there could still be a use for chariots, at least once more.

The army formed for the march—archers and cavalry, pikemen, lancers and knights, all ready—the baggage train alone called for thousands of pack animals to carry provisions required. Three days they remained encamped until fast riders changing horses in relays brought word the treasure train had reached the valley.

The army of Tzin poured upon the Jade Gate. Sitting on his shaggy mount, Casca watched the well-drilled men of his division with pride. In a short time he had turned them into the equals of the best the Emperor had to offer. Spurring Glam, he rode to the Emperor's tent and entered to be greeted by Li Tsao as she and her retinue were preparing to return to Ch'ang-an. Gliding to him with that well-remembered grace, she looked up into the face of the Roman, a somewhat quizzical expression playing around the corners of her mouth. Had Tzin told her of his condition?

Touching his chest with a long beautifully manicured nail, he heard her musical voice, "Well, ugly one, I see you have prospered. That is good. As you see, I have become more than I was also." She traced her nail along the scar on his face, standing close enough for him to smell the perfume of her breath. "We shall meet again, when we will have time to get to know each other better."

Casca felt his heart race and, taking a great gulp of air, shook his head. He then reported to the general staff and after a small argument as to the placement of his chariots in the column, the matter was settled to his satisfaction. He then returned to his troops and gave the order to take their places and begin the march.

Eighteen
BATTLE

Tzin often rode at Casca's side during the march to the Valley of Chong-Ye, where they would bivouac and wait for the word that the barbarians had gone for the bait. In the cool of the evenings, the King and his baron would spend time together. The youngster was fascinated by the Roman. His tale was one at which to marvel. He constantly posed questions to Casca, shaking his head at the stories the Roman told of the world beyond the wall and oceans. Tzin would cluck his tongue at the depths of ignorance of the rest of the world. True, the Romans and Greeks had made some modest attempt at culture and civilization, but to Tzin's mind, they were only a few degrees above the aboriginal tribes which infested the jungles of the southern empire.

Fast riders brought word that the tribes of the Hsuing-nu were on the march and already were near the road leading to the Valley of Chong-Ye, where the treasure train was encamped. The Hsuing-nu had merged into the two long columns which had flanked the swamp marshes of Chin-yo. Their out-riders were already at the entrance to the pass and had been seen scouting the high ground and even circled far to the rear, but they had not gone as far as the emperor's main force. They would return to their chieftains with the word the treasure was alone. With this information, only one fire a day would be permitted and the soldiers of the Empire would eat cold rations at night. There could be no chance of a campfire being spotted by a stray scout for the Hsuing-nu.

The army advanced to their final campsite, carefully hidden. The thousands of men were ordered to maintain strict silence and minimum movement. The deep valley in which they waited was ringed with a strong force of the fastest horsemen and best archers.

These men lay in places of concealment to stop any who might take word of their presence, be they barbarians or traitors. None would be permitted to approach the valley or leave it until the Emperor commanded otherwise. There was no more they could do, just wait. The waiting was always the worst, the tension gnawed at one's innards and made the constant droning of the flies unbearable. It was difficult to prevent outbreaks of temper and only the strictest punishment could serve as a deterrent. The day before ten men and their commander had been beheaded for fighting among themselves. The commander lost his head for allowing it to happen. The example served its purpose and the rest of the army and its officers knew what fate awaited them if they failed to keep proper discipline.

Constant communication was maintained between the treasure train and the army by a clever system of mirrors flashing coded signals over the twenty miles separating them. A signal of two bonfires would be lit at night if that was when the attack was to take place. Though Casca doubted that would occur. From what he had learned, the Hsuing-nu preferred the early hours of predawn. When wary men were still in their deepest sleep was the most likely time for them to hit; still, one never knew for certain and the precautions were taken.

The Hsuing-nu rode under standards of human heads and oxtails. Shamans cast bones and read the future; a great victory was to be had. From a distance they appeared to be a long line of ants crossing the marshes and entering the sheltered confines of the region of passes and valleys that led to the Jade Gate and the riches of Han beyond. A cloud of dust rose over them as they entered the drier regions where the marshes gave way to ever greater encroachments of the arid regions that sometimes would claim even the huge swamps.

Fierce men, they fed on a diet of meat and lust for blood as they rode. Grim brown faces that were strangers to any feeling of compassion or mercy. They lived for slaughter and died for it, this making no difference as it was a warrior's only honored ending.

Ten miles from the encampment of ten thousand men guarding the treasure train they massed each under their own tribes standard. The chieftains gathered in the felt yurt of the strongest tribes' leader, Longi, one of the oldest men of the tribes, who had survived more battles than most men would see in years. His teeth had long since been worn to stubs from the sand that found its way into everything they ate and had slowly ground the teeth down to the gums. His meat was prechewed by women of the tribe and meat was all he would eat, meat and blood from the veins of his herd of horses; only cattle ate that which grew from the ground.

In the smoky interior, the chieftains ate and listened to the words of the shamans. Tomorrow they would attack with the first light of the sky. They would ride down the defenders of the treasure with no need for tactics as this was to be a mass charge of the entire nation, one hundred thousand horsemen would trample all under their hooves. Each tribe was to select a thousand of their best warriors to form a unit of twenty thousand to strike straight to the treasure, while the rest finished off the imperial guard. They were also to insure the treasure found its way into the proper hands—namely, theirs.

That night they feasted long on meat and fermented mares' milk, gloating in the thought of the riches and slaughter that the morrow would bring. Before the red glow of the coming sun brought the false dawn, the army of Tzin was on the march in the cool of the predawn. They moved to the edge of the valley where the ten thousand waited with their Trojan Horse, behind a small rise. They were not able to be seen from the entrance from which the barbarians must come but still, strong pickets were set.

Casca's chariots were behind the first rank of cavalry, their reinsmen and archers curled up in their cloaks to catch a few more minutes of sleep. They knew the day would be long. In the camp of the Hsuing-nu the warriors massed under their standards while the shamans and chiefs made sacrifice to the sun. The shamans wailed and chanted, waiting for the moment when the sun would first show itself over the edge of the world, glowing red.

The shamans watched carefully, their victims bound between two horses, the cool of day sending shivers over them, long curved knives held expectantly and then. . .the *sun!* With a wail, they sliced open the stomachs of their victims, the stretching between the horses aiding in forcing the intestines out to the ground where they lay in slimy steaming mass of convoluted tissue. Quickly the shamans searched through them for any sign of an ill omen and finding none, they whipped the flanks of the horses and the bodies of the victims were torn in two. The horses raced around the camp, the torn cadavers bouncing behind. They cried out, "We ride! The horde rides!"

By the thousands they spilled like a flood into the entrance of the valley, whipping their beasts with the flat of their blades, racing low in the saddle and leaning over, they swept the first rank of the defenders under their hooves screaming with pleasure. Several halted long enough to take heads and hang them from their saddles before racing on.

In the valley center, the defenders were ready behind boulders and rocks. They waited. The crossbow men and infantry and cavalry formed one unit stretching across the valley and waited. They were not to attack, but to hold only so long as they could and then withdraw and break away, drawing the barbarians after them; at this moment, the main force of Tzin would enter the battle and the Hsuing-nu would be crushed. The only fly in the ointment was that the army of Kushan had not made its appearance. The Yueh-chih were delayed by rockslides and floods to the south of the Suget Pass and would not be here this day. So be it, the die was cast, they were seventy thousand to the barbarians' hundred thousand; close enough so that a surprise on their side should be more than enough.

The first wave of barbarians struck the main force of the treasure party, slicing deep into the ranks. They cut and slashed their way in, trying to reach the tents behind, which they knew held the gold their masters craved. Like demons they fought, each in his own world of blood. A thousand broke through to the rear and were cut down by the bolts from the hidden archers and crossbows. A hundred managed to fight their way back through the broken ranks of the soldiers of Tzin and rejoin their tribes. A blaring bugle call which signalled the ten thousand to begin their withdrawal fighting against the ever increasing numbers of savages who crowded in on them. A solid wall of screaming mindless killers, they withdrew; the pressure of the barbarians made it difficult to break away with any semblance of order.

Another bugle blast and it was each man for himself. The soldiers of Tzin broke and raced back into the valley, riding for their lives. The dogs of the steppes raced after them. Four thousand never made it and the survivors of the king rode for their lives.

The bugles also signalled the main army to advance. Sung Ti had not had much time to spend with Casca. As his aide-de-camp, he had much to prepare for and even now the last of the chains that had so carefully been forged in the furnaces of Chung Wei were being attached to the ring bolts of the chariots, a rope of iron stretched between them, the chariots were ready. Horses neighed and whinnied, the smell of blood coming to them on the morning breeze. Their eyes rolled in fear and uncertainty. Their masters' words and hands tried to soothe them.

The army stepped forth over the small rise. The land fell away from them. They would be attacking downhill. The division commanders waited and then the second bugle blast sounded, showing that the defenders were breaking ranks. They raised swords, cried, "Death to the barbarians! Long live the Son of Heaven!" and sixty thousand men and animals moved forward.

Casca positioned himself where he could watch not only his charioteers but the young king as well. The boy was eager and might get into trouble. The advancing forces of Tzin met those of the Hsuing-nu and for a moment hung suspended in the terrible confrontation. They were locked in a death grip none could escape; eight thousand men of Tzin died in less than ten minutes, but not before taking an equal amount of barbarians with them. The shock of meeting Tzin's reinforcements gave pause to the tribesmen. They halted, breathing deeply, the sides of their horses heaving.

A long low growling rose from them and in a spontaneous burst of hatred, they charged; horses shoulder to shoulder, a thousand across and behind packed deep with their brethren urging them on, trying to find their way into the front ranks, screaming and crying for blood.

The time came for the chariots to be used and the

reinsmen lined their war wagons up, the chains connecting each to the other in pairs. They looked to their leader. Casca drew his short sword and with a sweep pointed it to the battle. Three hundred chariots surged forth, slowly at first and then gaining speed they crashed into the living wall of tribesmen, the chains tearing the feet out from under the tribesmen's horses. By the hundreds, the animals fell to the sandy valley floor with broken legs, spilling their riders to the ground, where they were trampled under the hooves of their brothers or crushed under the wheels of the chariots. Over half of the three hundred chariots were swamped under the deluge of screaming tribesmen, but not before they had thrown the army of barbarians into a confused milling mass.

The orderly ranks of the imperial cavalry and infantry poured down on the confused tribesmen, slicing and striking, they performed great slaughter. Disciplined and efficient, they went about their soldiers' work.

The barbarians were beaten. The chariots had done their job. Now it was up to them to finish off as many as they could. From the corner of his eye, Casca saw the King slice the head off a Hsuing-nu chieftain and race into the battle followed by his personal household guard. He plunged into the milling knot of tribesmen, showing a total lack of concern for his own safety.

"Oh, shit. That little bastard's going to get himself in trouble," thought Casca. Turning over command of the remaining chariots to Sung Ti, he permitted him to join the battle, whipping Glam's shaggy carcass, fighting his way to the spot where the king had disappeared into the whirling mass of men, beasts and dust. Striking left and right, Casca laid about him whacking the hand off a tribesman who grabbed his reins and broke the neck of another with a well placed kick in the face. The king was down. His horse had its legs cut out from under it and lay screaming like a woman in that shrill manner only horses dying have. The surviving guards placed themselves in a circle around their imperial master ready to die rather than leave him; had their master died, they would live in disgrace and shame forever.

Driving his sword through the eye of a wild-faced barbarian, Casca broke through to the king. Glam rose on his hind legs and struck out with his sharp hooves, crushing the brain case of a wiry tribesman like an eggshell. The king's guard commander grabbed the imperial person and ignoring his lord's protests, threw him to Casca, who laid him across his saddle, holding him like a sack of grain. The commander cried out for Casca to save the king and Casca saw him go down as the last of the guard was overwhelmed and a tribesman severed the commander's spinal cord with a well-placed axe blow that broke him in two at the back.

Whirling Glam around, Casca fought his way back, ignoring Tzin's threats to have him made into an eunuch if he didn't let him down immediately. Slapping the youngster on the ass, Casca screamed above the din, "Keep still, my Lord, or you won't be able to give that command."

When they reached the rear of the battle, Casca deposited the young king unceremoniously at the feet of his generals. On the battlefield, the tribesmen began to waver, their confidence broken. Instead of the easy victory they had anticipated, they found an avenging army of disciplined, well trained troops and those damned chariots, that knocked the horses off their feet.

The bugles blared once more and the reserves were sent in. The influx of fresh troops was too much and the Hsuing-nu broke, fleeing in panic, back the way they had come, trampling any too slow to get out of their way under their hooves. They ran while the soldiers of the empire pursued and cut down all stragglers and wounded where they were found. No prisoners were taken as the Hsuing-nu made poor slaves and only a few were ever kept at any one time, mainly for stable duties.

Longi was found pinned under his horse and spat in the face of the young Tzin warrior who slit his throat.

If the forces of Kushan had been present, the Hsuing-nu would have been eliminated once and for all, but as it was, thirty thousand made their way back into the marshes and swamps. They would come again; someday they would ride out on the steppes again and wage war on the Chin, but for now, the young king had his victory.

In the battle, Casca had admired the technique of Sung Ti and his flashing blade, the use he made of long sweeping slashing strokes that changed in mid-air from a strike to the head, to a sideswipe that laid a barbarian's gut open. His stance and posture as he performed his martial ritual reminded Casca of Shiu Lao Tze, who had taught him the way of the open hand fighting so long ago. Yes, there was a definite resemblance. Sung Ti had created a new style, probably too difficult to teach the ordinary soldier, but who knows thought Casca, one day it might catch on.

Nineteen
LI TSAO

After Casca's rescue of his royal person, the Emperor Tzin insisted he leave his mountain domain and take personal command of the Imperial Guard. At Casca's suggestion, Sung Ti took his place as lord of Chung Wei. As a parting gesture, he also made a gift of Mei Cho to his comrade in arms. He had not failed to notice the looks that went between them and how she lowered her eyes as a flush would creep up to her face, when Sung Ti came around. The rude manner in which Mei Cho often treated Sung convinced Casca she had the hots for this dashing young warrior. Casca was never one to stand in the way of love and besides, he reasoned, she was a nice girl and deserved a chance at a normal life—something he would certainly never be able to give any woman.

Sung had been overcome at his friend's generosity and once Mei Cho's new position was made clear to her, he quickly put her in her place with a few sharp commands that had her crawling on her belly before him, completely submissive and content. The big nose had been kind to her but never really understood that to a woman like her, the only true pleasure she could have would be from a man who mastered her completely. The new Lord of Chung Wei was of her people and understood the proper manner of gaining her love.

Casca left the two, well pleased with their fortune and rode to the royal city where he donned the colors of the Imperial Guard—black and gold silk robes set about with a red sash. The next nine years flew by rapidly and several times he and the emperor ventured forth to do battle against the tribes beyond the wall. As the young king grew older and wiser in the ways of war, he became ever more attached to his foreign lord and servant. Twice more the Roman saved his ass when in his eagerness, Tzin put his own life in jeopardy. They worked well together and often shared moments in the gardens where Tzin would try to give Casca some of the feelings of the people of Chin and their love of art and beauty. No people on the face of the earth were so completely devoted to beauty in all its forms, from the lowest peasant to the highest lord all tried to acquire what little share of beauty they could.

The most beautiful of all the possessions of Tzin was the lady Li Tsao, who grew more lovely with each year, growing into a full woman, confident in her mind and body. She controlled the emperor and was his first consort to the neglect of all others. She was his only constant companion and advisor. True, he, occasionally as men will, took off with Casca for a couple of nights of hell raising with the fine and talented courtesans of his empire, but always he returned to Li Tsao. His only sadness was her failure to bear him a son. Casca kept his distance from her. There was always the feeling in the back of his mind that she was dangerous in the way only the female of any species can be and noted she watched him as the years went by. Several times when they met she would look closely at his face, a slight look of consternation behind her almond eyes as if troubled by something she saw and couldn't put her finger on.

The Hsiung-nu gave them no more trouble, but the other tribes were growing in strength and constantly trying their luck at raping the soft lands behind the wall, only to be met with steel instead of silk. Tzin knew well the value of his army and they served him well. If only he could unite the eastern empire under his cousins he might be able to provide the final solution for the security of Han. But this was not to be. His cousin insisted on hiring tribesmen from the Hsien-pi in lieu of his own people. Like the Romans in their use of the barbarians of Germany and the gothic kingdoms, they bred the seeds of their own destruction.

Sung sent word that he and the woman Mei Cho had a son and if it would please him, they would like to name the child after Casca, though the pronunciation would be slightly different in their language. Casca was present before the priests and family when the child was raised over his father's head and it was announced that from that day on he would be known as Ch'saca Sung Ti. Casca assumed the role of godfather to the child by presenting the offerings of incense and rice to the gods and ancestors of Tsung Ti and taking the small blade which Tsung had given him, he laid it on the child's naked body. Sung cried out joyfully when the child's fat fingers wrapped themselves around the hilt and held it firmly in his baby's grasp.

"A good sign, Lord Casca. He will be a great warrior and joy to his family."

Mei Cho had blossomed in her delivery of a man child and her figure and face had filled out to a ripeness that gave her a glow. She knelt before the man who had been her master and touched her head to his boot.

"Thank you, Big Nose," she whispered in words only he could hear, "thank you. My life is full."

After his return to Ch'ang-an, he kept himself busy with the training of the guard, but time was against him. Tzin knew his secret, that time would soon be on him and he must leave. His commanders and men grew old and retired to farms and estates to raise families but the silver in their beards never came to Casca.

Li Tsao watched.

In the garden where the two rocks had been tied so long ago by the ancient poet, she found him sitting on the same bench where he had first met the emperor. Gliding over the stone pathway, the beams of the moon shone through the petals of the blossoming fruit trees and flowers. Sitting beside him she looked closely at his face.

"What is your secret, ugly one?"

The question shocked him for a moment. He tried to collect his thoughts and then stammering said: "I have no secret. I am just a common soldier, content to serve our master."

Li Tsao waved a graceful hand. "No lies, Barbarian. I am a woman grown and even in my hair I have found silver traces of time, but you are the same as when we met on the Silk Road. There is no change in you. Not any. You are the same in body and appearance as you were then. Why do you not age? Tell me and there is nothing in this land that cannot be yours."

She moved closer to him, her face only inches from his, the smell of her perfume sweeping over him. Her words like a silk sword, she again repeated, "There is nothing in this land which may not be yours—gold, slaves, power. . ." She ran her lacquered nails along the thin scar of his face "even myself. I could show you pleasures you have not dreamed of. I can be all things to you and teach you the sensations of pleasure only a few in this world have ever experienced. Tell me, what is your secret. A potion, a magic ritual that keeps you young? This I must know. Is it bathing in the blood of young virgins? I have tried that myself but it has failed. Tell me and we shall share all that is here forever. I can make you King."

Firmly, Casca took her small hand in his own and began to squeeze gently at first and then increasing pressure until a gasp of pain broke from her perfect lips. For the first time, Casca knew the reality of what she was and the cruelty that lay behind the smiles and graceful manner. Her beauty and youth were all that were important to her. All else was expendable, including Tzin.

Barely able to control his anger, his throat

tightened. "Get away from me, bitch. There is nothing I can give or tell you. Keep away from me."

Releasing her hand, the new flow of blood to her fingers made her tingle as the pressure of his scarred hand released hers. Rising he walked away, turning back to look at her sitting quietly in the moonlight.

Li Tsao smiled sweetly, "You shouldn't have done that, ugly one." She rose and then disappeared into the shadows of the garden.

The next few weeks, Casca kept a wary eye on the king's consort, shocked at the depths of cruelty that lay beneath that delicate exterior. Not since Salome had he known a woman as evil as this. Whenever they met, she would smile and be graceful, her manners and words always polite, always correct without a hint of the hate that lay beneath her bosom. No one had ever refused her. She vowed the ugly barbarian would know what it meant to deny her that which she desired above all else—eternal youth and beauty.

The business of the empire went on. In the fall Tzin left Ch'ang An to visit some of the southern provinces. It was good policy and occasionally he showed himself to the people and passed judgements in person. While he was gone, his lady sat in his stead, governed the city and several times gave formal parties and banquets.

Always Casca refused to attend, pleading pressing matters of the army requiring him to be elsewhere. But one invitation came which he could not refuse. Sung Ti, Mei Cho and their son were ordered to the capitol. Li Tsao had received permission from the emperor to confirm the House of

Tsung-ti in their position as lords of Chung Wei and that the line from this time henceforth would be hereditary to be passed on to the young boy Ch'asca, the barbarian's godson. For this occasion, Casca had to attend and witness the confirmation of hereditary nobility.

Young Ch'asca was a fine boy who even now could sit a saddle and ride his pony with the same élan of his father. Five was a great age for a child when all was new and wonderful and Casca envied his friend his son.

Following the official confirmation, the lesser nobles bowed and acknowledged the position of nobility of Sung Ti. Gifts were presented and the banquet held in the larger imperial gardens.

Casca sat with his godson on his knee, letting the boy ride his leg like a mountain pony while Li Tsao smiled and performed the duties of a hostess to the gathering of nobles and warriors. The banquet lasted long with one exotic course of food following another. Snow had even been brought from the distant mountains to chill the rare wines and beverages. The changing hues of the trees gave the final touch of color to this joyous occasion.

Calling for a toast to the honor of the new family, the guests' cups were filled with fine white wine of the south. All drank deeply. Casca swallowed one long draught and raised his empty cup to his friend.

"Long life and honor to the Tsung-Ti and his son, who will one day be Baron of Chung Wei."

The last words stuck in his throat as a coldness gripped his limbs and spread over his entire body stiffening it. He turned to look at Li Tsao and tried to raise an accusing finger but was unable, the coldness reached his brain and claimed him. His body had not hit the ground before Li Tsao gave a curt order and the slave who had filled his cup found his head suddenly separated from his body, lying on the ground waiting for the rest of him to fall. The guard who had performed the execution looked expectantly at the Imperial Lady and licked his lips in anticipation of the reward she had promised. That night, he too, would join his ancestors before he ever knew the pleasures of her arms.

Twenty
THE BURIAL

The procession wound its way through the sculptured valleys and terraced hills leading to the place of entombment. Peasants bowed low in Kowtow before the symbols of the Imperial Lady. Her palanquin cast reflected rays of light from the gold leaf and polished lapis lazuli which made up the intertwined dragons and seemed to be lending their sinuous strength to the columns supporting the silken canopy beneath which Lady Li Tsao reclined.

Her face was like ivory which had turned gold with time, beautiful but unfeeling: only in the almond eyes were hints of deeper passion and desires.

Behind, came the litter bearing Casca's coffin of teakwood, embellished with scenes of his service to the Emperor. Inside, Casca lay on silk cushions, his arms tied to his sides and a silk gag covering his mouth. Wailers and singers led the way; musicians followed, lending the beat of brass gongs and flutes to the lilting voices of the paid mourners. This was indeed a noble's funeral.

Guards escorting the party marched in solemn dignity prodigious in the apparel of the Imperial Protectors—black on gold and a circle of gold thread in which was the ideograph of the Emperor Tzin—marching in half-step, their pikes lowered to forward angle position, decreed for a solemn occasion such as this. They were paying homage to a brave and fallen soldier. Most had fought alongside him at one time or another.

The day was clear and sharp with only a hint of the coming north winds in the light breeze, causing pennants and flags on the pikes and standards to whip, gently fluttering. The procession itself, from a distance, appeared to depict one of the scenes that the artisans of Chin delighted so much in preserving on painstakingly carved tusks of ivory and on jade. The rice paddies and tamarisk trees added background to this touching act of affection and honor that Lady Li Tsao was paying a friend of the Son of Heaven, Emperor Tzin.

A languid wave of her hand silenced the wailers and musicians. They had reached the place of entombment. The porters stood breathing deeply though the day was cool, the weight of the coffin and palanquin giving them a sweaty glistening sheen to their faces.

Between the clefts of a rocky gorge, the tomb had been built. The walls and sides of carefully joined gray stone were sealed with a mixture of lime and rock dust to make it airtight. The gaping tomb awaited its occupant. A great slab of stone bearing the Imperial Seal showed this was an honored tomb and not to be disturbed.

Casca was motionless in his coffin. The drugs administered earlier served to keep him quiet; though not unconscious, he was unable to move or talk. His mind tried to reach out from the darkness. It seemed almost as if he could see what was happening in a detached way, as if he were watching from the heights of one of the nearby hills. The litter bearers lowered their burden to the earth and stepped away. The guards took positions indicated by their commander and turned their backs to the tomb, facing outward. The priests lit sticks of joss and incense, placing them on the tomb and spinning their prayer wheels: they too, turned away from the tomb.

Li Tsao and her two personal physicians approached the casket. She stood by idly, enjoying the strengthening warmth of the fall sun as it neared midday. The two healers opened the lid of the teak casket, exposing Casca to the sky. His head was on silk pillows and his bindings concealed by robes of honor. Only the silken gag was visible, appearing to be more of a covering for his lower face than anything else.

Waving the physicians away, Li Tsao moved with the grace of a temple dancer, her small delicate body swaying slightly with each tiny step, her fan of thinnest ivory sheaves making gentle breezes. Casca's eyes were closed. Li Tsao leaned over, her brown eyes taking in the face of one who had denied her the right to eternal youth. She was beautiful still, but time's insidious advance could not be stopped forever. One day the artful use of cosmetics would no longer be able to hide the small lines now making their slow but sure appearance on her ivory skin, marring the once perfect beauty.

Snapping her fingers, an attendant approached bringing an object wrapped in white silk. Taking it from him and then waving a hand of dismissal, she laid the silken package on the chest of Casca.

"Barbarian, do you hear me?" Taking his cheek between her lacquered nails she twisted once, and then again, leaving a bloody trickle running down his face. Casca's eyes opened slowly, blurred from the drug-induced sleep. He tried to focus with difficulty. "Good, Barbarian, I have brought you something," she patted the silk package. "In here is your sword. You may need it to fight your way through the demons of darkness. I felt much for you, but you rejected me and this cannot go unpunished, but for the feelings and the life we might have had eternally young, I leave you your weapon." Her face swam above him as she leaned over and kissed him long and full on the mouth, her tongue darting like a serpent. She kissed him as she would one she loved long and full, as if in this final kiss she was trying to draw off the essence that made him what he was. Placing her fingers over his face, she closed his eyes, her voice lilting and sweet she whispered, "Sleep the long sleep of eternity."

Darkness closed in again as the lid of his coffin was closed and even the thin glow of light from the sun through his shut lids was terminated. The slaves lowered Casca into the rock tomb that would be his home for the ages. Straining, they needed the help of twenty guards to place the massive slab on top.

They bowed their way back from the tomb, out of sight. This was the business of those above them as they were above the vermin that crawled in the bowels of the earth.

One by one, the soldiers made obeisance and lit sticks of incense for the deceased and laid them on the small stone altar where the incense burned. The priests began their death chant in earnest, nasally whining paeans to the dark spirits to let the traveler through safely to join his ancestors. The mourners—the best that money could buy and completely devoted to their occupation—took their cue and began to wail as if a child had been torn away from them. With undulating cries of grief and sorrow, they pitched themselves into ever greater expressions of grief, slashing their faces with their fingernails and tearing their clothes into shreds to the syncopation of the gongs and flutes until they lay exhausted upon the ground in a sobbing mass of genuine bereavement.

Thus, Casca was buried.

The procession re-formed itself and left quietly with dignity. The Lady Li Tsao being well-pleased made a mental note to use the same mourners when the Emperor died. Calling her attendant, she asked to which guild they belonged.

Casca awoke, the effects of the opiate having worn off; most men would have been unconscious for at least a full day and night. The procession had not yet reached the outskirts of the sacred city when the terror came over him. Unable to move his arms, the darkness enveloped him like some horrible placenta.

"No!" he screamed through muffled lips. "No!"

The terror of being buried alive washed over him. The same desperate fear he had felt as a slave in the mines of Greece returned. To be buried alive, unable to die. *How long would the darkness last . . . one year . . . five . . . a hundred or for eternity?*

He cried out through his gag, his mouth working at the bindings. He beat his head against the silken pillows in anguish. "*Alive, the bitch has buried me alive.*" The horror settled on him giving vent to an icy chill that came from the surface of his skin, deep into his bones. "*Alive, for how long? How can I find the Jew if I'm buried here forever.*" Casca's efforts to free himself slackened. He felt heavy, his arms and legs like lead appendages, his chest aching for air. The darkness came again, his eyes closed once more and the deep chill faded. Casca was still, his body unmoving. Then a tiny movement in the great vein of his neck. Minutes passed . . . then another quick twitch of the large vein. Once every twenty minutes his pulse beat and every forty minutes his chest would move slowly, taking a shallow breath. His system came to an almost complete halt. Like the great bears of the ice mountains, Casca slept.

The years passed, the business of the kingdom went on, babes were born, old men died and wars were fought. Occasionally a bundle of fresh incense would be lit at his grave by one with whom he had soldiered. Bowls of rice to feed his spirit were set with honor. The birds and rats appreciated the offerings. Occasionally one of the great plates of the earth shifted and tremors came to the surface as minor quakes, not severe or uncommon in this land. To the peasant, this was accepted like the seasons—

some were good and some were bad—but all were part of their life.

Casca's tomb cracked open at the north seam, letting in a tiny amount of air; not much, but enough for the sleeping one inside. With the crack came others. Smaller vermin and insects made homes in the robes of silk, families grew in the beard and chest hair of the sleeper. His hair still grew and in the growth were many colonies of worms, seeking the warmer spots in his armpits a small family of vipers chose the place between his crotch for their own. The insects and a minute amount of moisture weakened the fabric of the robes and bindings until finally, a great rat made his way in after gnawing for days at the crack. The rodent walked up and down the length of Casca carefully to avoid the snakes and after satisfying himself, took a bite out of Casca's big toe but immediately began to eat dirt and run his mouth and tongue over the ground trying to get the taste out. This was a large piece of meat and the rat prided himself on being able to eat anything, but not this—to eat this was death. In frustrated hunger, the rat nibbled and chewed the silk bindings away from Casca's arms and while trying to digest his silk meal, became a meal himself for a family of snakes in the sleeper's crotch.

Twenty-One
THE PREACHER

The seasons came and went in their time. The sleeper in his bed of stone was unaware of the years passing. Only the endless weaving of the brown spider marked the passage of the years as she spun a gossamer web over the still form of the sleeping man, covering him from head to feet in a delicate pattern of webs in which she trapped smaller insects to feed her brood. When she died, others took her place, spinning their own silken threads until the sleeper appeared to be more of a giant embryonic larva waiting in his cocoon for time to hatch. Beneath the rocks, the earth periodically shifted and shuffled, causing tremors on the surface. The year's frost killed the blossoming cherry tree buds by the hillside and for another three weeks, the branches were bare, but spring finally came, as she must. The winds blew gently over the grass and the peasants in the fields labored planting; their backs bent early from constant stooping as they painstakingly strived to make the earth produce the necessities for their existence.

The planting of the peasants was broken by the sound of a bell ringing. They stopped, turning their heads to the sound from the hillside. A figure made its way down to the field, a staff in one hand, and in the other, a bell of bronze which he rang with every other step. An unintelligible chanting issued from the scarecrow caricature that came closer into view; a foreigner and one touched by the gods, obviously mad and therefore blessed.

The peasants waited, their faces in the shadows of the woven straw conical-shaped hats worn by men and women alike, their legs encrusted with dried mud to above the knees. They waited to see what the stranger wanted.

"Peace and the blessing of the Messiah on you," spoke the stranger in Chinese. "Praise God, you heathen, for I bring to you the greatest gift of the world; the word of the living God and salvation awaits those who will listen and heed. Bow your heads you heathen dogs." The mad man pointed one gnarled finger at Wing Sung, the man in whose fields the others toiled: "Down you slant-eyed barbarian and I shall save your soul, though I don't know why the Lord has placed this burden on me." His voice rose to a moderate bellow: "Down!"

Startled, Wing Sung obeyed. After all one never knew about these mad monks who wandered the earth, for did not Buddha do much the same? It was considered unwise to offend those the gods had touched and unlucky, especially during the seasons of planting when all luck is needed. If he's just a madman, we will stone him to death later; for now, it's best to play it safe.

Wing Sung's laborers followed his action. All

bowed low from the waist, wondering what was going to happen next.

The madman strode toward them, his clothes a nondescript mixture of castoff items from a dozen tribes; though just which, by this time, none could tell. His beard reached to his waist and a look of blind fanaticism was clear in his red-rimmed eyes.

"I am Peter. I have come to you at the bidding of the Lord Jesus Christ, for in my dreams he commanded me to go forth and save souls of those who have not heard his words. Fifteen years I have wandered and preached the gospel to the benighted heathen and always the Lord has provided, though not as well as I would have liked sometimes—indeed, I have lost more pounds than I started with, but I am well enough and if the Lord chooses to test me, who am I to question Him?" The question was as much to himself as to anyone else and as it did not require an answer, he continued, "Now, you sloe-eyed idol worshippers, you are in luck today, because today and today only, I am going to bring to some salvation and eternal life in paradise. Those of you who are so ignorant as not to recognize the truth of my words will just have to go to Hell and that's fine with me. I will have given you a chance and it's your tough luck if you pass it up."

Wing Sung peered up through the epicanthic folds of his eyes. "Are you from the lands to the west?" he queried, still not certain if the stranger was blessed or just nuts.

"Indeed I am, you poor miserable idolater. I have come from a land called Dacia. There I heard the words of the Gospel and knew I was to bring the Lord's word to all within range of my voice," his eyes flashed as he recalled his own salvation, "I learned your tongue while living with a tribe of nomads in the great desert where I saved many souls for the Lord. Now, which of you wishes to be saved first? Step forward, don't be bashful. I don't have all day you know."

Wing Sung kept his opinions to himself but addressed the madman once more. "Holy man, there is another of your own race entombed nearby, a great warrior who served the Emperor Tzin. He was put into the great stone sarcophagus there," pointing to the nearby valley where the tomb of Casca lay.

Peter the madman looked to the place where Wing Sung had pointed. "A man of my race you say? Was he a Christian?"

"What's a Christian?" Wing Sung asked.

"A Christian is a follower of the crucified God, Christ." Then showing Wing Sung what the Chinese considered a particularly gruesome item, a small silver crucifix with a man nailed to it, Wing Sung shrugged. "I don't know if he was what you call a Christian or not, but he was entombed with honors due a noble of the royal court by the Lady Li Tsao, consort to the Emperor Tzin."

Peter drew himself up to his full height, his bony cheeks flushed with the thought he might be able to save a soul. "Why you miserable heathen, if he was buried by your idol-worshipping practices, he will never know paradise. The least I can do is say the last rites over him to give his soul a chance for salvation. Show me the way."

Wing Sung did as he was told and showed the ragged messenger of the one called the Messiah to the place of Casca's entombment. The villagers gathered in the background, anxious to see what this weird ragged, pale-faced stranger would do. They squatted in a semicircle, their knees almost to their chest and waited.

Peter, full of righteous fervor approached the tomb. Standing before it he saw the embossed emblems of eternal life and the four-toed dragon, given only to those of the royal household and the tree of life with spreading branches. Raising his silver crucifix, he began to chant and preach, his voice gaining strength as he got into his act. His eyes raised, body twitching, he gained power such as he had never known. The power was on him. His voice echoed throughout the hills and valleys. He got into his thing as he spoke the words of the gospel and finally the words of Revelation.

Nature picked this particular time to let the mountainous rocky plates beneath the earth shift once more, the shock from below traveling to the surface like a stone in a lake rippling its way out in widening circles, cracking the granite boulders into splinters and changing the course of an underground hot spring; the one that fed the baths of the village of Feng Shang. The vibrating waves of the earthquake cracked further the stone tomb, letting the boiling waters of the hot spring flow into the interior, cooking all the assorted vermin that had chosen to make Casca and his tomb their home. Rats as well as spiders, died in a steam that would have driven Casca mad with pain had he been able to feel the heat. The waves of the earthquake reached the surface, the ground swaying as if at sea.

Peter, totally involved with orations, feeling filled with the power of the Spirit of the Lord, took the earthquake to be a manifestation of the Lord's power. He filled his lungs and bellowed even louder, while the peasants, terrified, scurried for higher ground, leaving the madman to his magic. Peter cried out in fanatic fervor:

"*And the earth shall give up her dead!*"

At that moment, Casca's tomb opened. The huge covering stone split down the center, the sides buckled into dusty fragments as clouds of steam poured forth, the earth roared and stones shrieked as they were torn apart—the steam, shocks and air let into the tomb bringing Casca back to awareness.

Peter was really getting off on his sermon when in the center of the steam cloud issuing from the ruptured tomb, a figure stepped out.

Casca, back from the dead and mad as hell, came out of the steam and dust from his wrecked sarcophagus, hair past his shoulders and an even rattier beard reaching to his chest, dead insects in matted knots from his face and hair. The silken robes long since had turned into rotting fragments of their former glory and hung in web-matted shreds. A dead rat dropped from one of the sleeve folds. It had been parboiled and so was Casca, his skin a bright cherry red with pale blisters the size of wine cups standing out. His sword in his hand, Casca was ready to kick ass and take names. The steam and the air, along with the vibrations of the earthquake had restored him and with awakening came instant remembrance. Casca was pissed. The earth gave one more spasmodic surge, heaving several trees up by the roots and then was still.

Peter froze, his mouth hanging open at the apparitions that had come forth at his words *And the earth shall give up her dead*.

"A miracle," he cried, his eyes filling with tears that he should be blessed with power from the Lord

Jesus Christ to restore the dead to life. He always knew that he would be rewarded for his piety, but this was more than he had ever dreamed of.

Holding his crucifix high above him, he rang the bell at Casca as he approached crying: "Blessed be the name of the Lord. On your knees and pray."

Casca ignored him.

"On your knees heathen," he repeated, "It isn't every day you're brought back from the valley of the dead."

Casca strode on, bits of cloth dropping from him leaving a trail of silk and bugs behind, and faced the mad preacher. Peter shook his cross in Casca's face and rang his bell even harder. Reaching over, Casca took the bell from Peter's hand and whacked him across the head with it, laying Peter out cold. The preacher lay spread out on the ground, his cross in the dust. Casca gave both a look of distaste and grumbled through cracked lips, "That damned bell was giving me a headache."

Ignoring the prone body of Peter, Casca moved off still grumbling to himself, and peeling strips of burned skin from his face and arms, stripping off his rags as he walked until finally he was naked, carrying only his sword. . .the sword that Lady Li Tsao had been gracious enough to place in the tomb with him. Spying the fields, Casca made for them and the village beyond.

"Food," he thought, "I need something to eat, anything." His scarred hide had turned almost fish-white during the years of his confinement; only the multitude of scars were lighter in color.

Walking through the deserted streets, there were some signs of minor damage from the quake, but nothing of any import. Wing Sung and the others had taken to their homes when they saw him approach. Whoever the preaching madman was, he certainly had some strange powers.

Smelling cooking rice, Casca entered the third house on the dirt street and walked in, scaring the crap out of the family living there. The mother hid her three children behind her while the father screwed up enough courage to face the pale, parboiled, bug-infested intruder. Performing Kowtow, he bowed low almost bent double in front of Casca and said quivering, "Please lord, we are poor people here and have nothing but the rags we wear and a few grains of rice to eat." Noticing Casca eyeing the cookpot where their dinner was simmering over a charcoal brazier, he hastily scooped out a large bowl and proffered it to the walking deadman.

Casca grunted his thanks between mouthfuls, choking the food down as fast as he could and swallowing water from a handy pitcher. The rice set like cement in his gut, but it was there and soon he began to feel more human. He smiled at the frightened family and spoke for the first time now that his throat was lubricated.

"Thanks and don't be frightened of me," he said in Chinese, "I am no devil or deadman come to life." Knowing the superstitions of the people, he thought it better to feed them a fairy tale.

"I was not dead when I was buried. No. A spell was put on me by a witch and I have slept until the earth set me free." Twisting the silver ring from his finger, he gave it to his host, "Here, this is for your food. Would you also find some clothes large enough to fit me?"

The excited peasant scurried away to do as he was asked, going immediately to the house of Wing

Sung where he told him what had transpired. The only omission was the gift of the silver ring, now hidden in his waistband: That one piece of silver was enough to buy a young cow and make him a man of means.

Wing Sung quickly found a robe for the stranger. He wanted no part of him. He ordered the peasant to take the robe and go, saying when such strange things happened, this usually meant no good for the common people.

Casca's reluctant host brought him the robe which was a little snug around the shoulders and arms but would serve. Casca put a pack of food under his arm, thanked his host and left. The day was still young enough for him to get some miles down and besides. . .he had a score to settle.

The preacher, on regaining consciousness, nursed his aching head and wondered why, when he was given the power to raise the dead, the first person raised had to be crazy. Coming to a rapid decision, he decided to leave this land and head back to the civilized lands of Rome and the Empire where a saint would be properly appreciated. He couldn't wait to show his new power to some of those stuffy smart-ass hermits who felt so smug in their lousy holes and caves meditating and praying.

"By God, they would sit up and take notice now."

Picking up his bell, he rang it a few times tentatively and then stopped putting it in his belt. Maybe the resurrected one wasn't so crazy after all. . .that damned bell could give a person a headache.

Twenty-Two
PUNISHMENT

Casca stood before the king dressed in the robes of the Imperial Guard which he had worn for so many years—black and gold silk, a red sash around his waist—his sword hung from a halberd resting on his left side. Tzin, Emperor of the West Kingdoms, shook his head in amazement at the tale Casca related. Casca did not tell him all the details, only that the Lady Li Tsao sitting by his Imperial Majesty's side had given him a potion which feigned death and he had laid in his coffin for almost eight years.

Tzin shook his head sadly from side to side and looked at his still beautiful Li Tsao, her face like aged porcelain, almost golden with only a few lines to tell of the years. She alone knew the effort it took to keep her appearance youthful. Her body was still as firm as that of a young maid. Looking back, Tzin saw Casca standing in the uniform in which they had fought together, side by side against the Huns and other barbarian tribes beyond the wall. He remembered the times this blue-eyed stranger had saved his life and his kingdom. He straightened his back, anger beginning to rise, some of the old élan returned, for he had been a warrior and man of honor. Hissing between his teeth, he faced Li Tsao pointing a jewel-encrusted finger at her.

"Witch", his eyes narrowed to small slits of rage, "you dare to cast your spells on one of my men. . .one who has served me well." He stood holding his scepter in his left hand. Li Tsao cringed, never had he spoken to her in anger. She had always been able to control him with her body and her mind. "Witch, you shall pay," he turned to the audience in attendance, raising his scepter, "Li Tsao is no more. She is as one dead in dishonor. Let none speak her name henceforth on pain of death." Motioning to his guards, he ordered her confined to her rooms until he decided her punishment.

Li Tsao started to speak but was interrupted by a curt imperial, "Silence. Speak not, or I shall have your tongue torn out by the roots before you leave this room. You are dead to all here and the dead do not speak."

Li Tsao straightened, her head erect she shook off the hand of the house guard and walked alone ahead of him. She was still a woman of consequence and pride and would let none here say they saw her weaken. That was one satisfaction she would not give those who gloated over her tragedy. There was still a good chance she could bring the Emperor around if she could just have a moment alone with him. She knew the weakness he had for her body and used the arts of love to such great effectiveness that he only took a concubine as a replacement when she was in her moon.

Descending from his Peacock Throne, the Emperor of the West Kingdoms, conqueror of the Huns and Son of Heaven, put his arms around Casca and embraced him. The audience bowed to their faces; never had they seen such an honor given. It was unheard of, undreamed of.

"Hear me. This man is a friend and ally. All shall honor him as they would me. He is elevated to Keeper of the Throne, right hand to myself, the Son of Heaven and your master. Let all pay homage to the Baron of Khitai."

Kowtow was performed as all prostrated themselves again and again, hissing between their teeth at the honor being shown the foreigner. The Emperor continued, "I have been blinded by the witch myself and know of the evil she has done, but in my passion I paid no heed and that is my sin. Now old friend, what will you have as compensation? Name it. Anything that is in this land is yours and if it be your wish, I will adopt you and you shall succeed me on the Throne of Heaven, even before the seed of my loins, should I have a son. I am sure that the reason I have no son now is the work of the witch. Tell me, is it your wish to be King when I go to join my ancestors?"

Glancing around the room, Casca caught varying looks from the faces of the nobles present, ranging from pleasure to jealous hatred. Casca looked his friend in the eye: "No lord, I wish nothing other than a good horse and if you see fit, my back pay. I believe it is time for me to go on. To try to rule in your stead would be a mistake for I have not your ability to rule a great empire. I am no more than what I was when first we met. So, with your permission, I have a desire to see my homeland again. But what of Li Tsao? Even though she is evil, I wouldn't want to think of her dying under the executioner's blade."

Tzin smiled enigmatically, "Have no fear on that part my friend. She will not go under the axe; indeed, no hand will touch her in violence. She will be punished, but the punishment will come from herself and her own mind. Now, if you would leave us, the road is open and while you travel in my lands, all must give you every assistance that you desire. You are a Baron of Khitai and shall so remain so long as you choose to remain in our lands."

Summoning the palace steward, a wizened elder known for his niggardliness with the royal purse strings, the Emperor commanded, "Wu Chingwah, give the Lord Casca all that he desires and do not stint. Let him have the pick of an animal from our stables and see that papers are prepared to give him royal messenger status so that he may have fresh mounts from our stables anywhere in the Empire."

Wu Chingwah bowed his obedience and beckoned Casca to follow him. As they left, Emperor Tzin gave his old comrade one long look, "Live long and well, Lord Casca. . .live long. . ."

The Roman bowed low and left the presence of the Son of Heaven. "Longer than you think old friend, much longer."

Li Tsao screamed repeatedly, covering her eyes. Kneeling on the carpeted floor, she screamed once more in terror. . .the terror of her own mind.

The Emperor's word was law and as he commanded, so it was done.

She screamed again, her sobbing racked with agony, remembering the Emperor's words: "No hand shall touch her. Her punishment shall be of her own making. Her beauty is the thing she values most and for this has tried to fight time and remain forever young. Long were the hours she spent in front of her mirrors, pleased with what she saw. Therefore, to her heart's contentment, she shall see herself. . ."

Li Tsao struggled to her knees. Naked, her face streaked with tears, she saw herself endlessly, repeated a thousand times. Her image looked back at her from the innumerable mirrors surrounding her. Nowhere could she escape her reflection. The room was to be lit constantly; never in darkness. Every waking moment she must look at herself without clothes and make-up, or dyes to keep the grey from her hair and every day she would see each tiny line and wrinkle grow longer and deeper with the passage of time. Unable to escape, Li Tsao screamed a cry that settled into an animal-like whimper and her reflections in their thousands cried also, an endless progression of images, forever.

The long ride from the heartland of the Empire of Tzin to the Great Wall was, even with the best of mounts the empire could offer, tedious. Everywhere the seal of the king was obeyed without question. Before the seal governors of provinces would bow low and perform obeisance, hissing between their teeth. As the Son of Heaven commanded, so it would be done. Casca was given the best of all the land had to offer. Sewn into the linings of his robes were two bags; one of gold, the other of jewels, the Emperor's parting gift to his loyal friend. In those small bags was enough wealth to last an ordinary man a lifetime. Feeling the bag of gems bounce against his leg he wondered, "A normal man a lifetime, but for me how long?"

Villages and cities became fewer as he neared the frontier until only the armed garrison outposts of the empire were to be found. The Wall stretching out as far as the eye could see and beyond, past the horizon, over mountains and through valleys. In comparison, Hadrian's Great Wall in Britannia was the effort of a child. Winding his way through the rocky passes and gorges between twisted pines and brush, he came to what the people of Khitai believed to be the end of the civilized world. Beyond the wall was only terror and man–beasts who preyed on their own, brutes less than human.

Casca approached the garrison where there were two thousand men whose job it was to watch the wall and patrol its length until they joined the next garrison to the east of them and the west. They would stay on the wall two years and then be replaced by others. The wall, like many of the minds of Khitai, seemed to be the barrier between good and evil, culture and barbarism.

Sung Mi Hsiung, Commander of the Garrison of The Jade Gate welcomed his guest, anxious to serve and honor the friend of the Son of Heaven, but Casca was driven by an inexplicable urgency. With a fresh mount—Hsiung's own horse—the gate was unbarred and he stepped forth. The great plains were empty. For a thousand and more leagues there were no men. The eastern Huns had been destroyed in their last great battle with Casca and the Emperor. The remnants of the tribes were only a few sad nomadic villages that tried to keep as much distance between the Land of the Han and themselves as was possible; some had gone so far as the Land of Eternal Ice.

Kicking his steed in the flanks, Casca rode first at a trot, then a gallop and at last a run, spurring the bay gelding on, racing onto the plains until only common sense made him stop, else the animal's heart would surely burst from the strain.

The sun was beginning its period when the golden chariot would be given rest and Apollo would sleep until the dawn. The West. Where were the rest of the Huns? For many years there had been a trickle of them to the edges of the empire. Some were hired as mercenaries by the Emperor of Rome, but where were the rest of the hoards?

The sun set red and huge, laying a rose-colored glow over the land bathing the endless prairies stretched before him. Somewhere out there. . .they are out there and have only one way to go. What was the saying, 'all roads lead to Rome.' They will come one day—the Huns will come by the thousands and the tens of thousands—they will come and Rome will cry.

The last red glow of the sun slid off the plumed and lacquered helmet of the Baron of Khitai, conqueror of the Eastern Huns, defender of the Peacock Throne. The blackness set in as the last rays faded on the man riding west.

Darkness covered the scar-faced, blue-eyed

Roman. . .CASCA, THE WAR LORD.

Goldman snapped out of it. Once more he had that feeling of being drained. Without looking, he knew that Casca had gone.

"God dammit, won't that bastard ever hang around long enough to answer a few questions?"

With a trembling hand, he poured himself a large shot of Jack Daniels Sour Mash Bourbon and swallowed the hot sweet whiskey, letting it settle into his stomach. The book of Machiavelli lay open on the table. Picking it up, he put it back into its place on the shelf. Pouring another drink, he sat in the overstuffed leather chair and raised the glass in a toast.

"Here's to you, you miserable bastard . . .wherever you are."

He walked with the tread of a man infinitely weary. . .a taxi came by from dropping off a couple of late night party-goers and stopped for the man on the street—might as well get one last fare before heading to the barn.

Casca settled himself into the seat, huddled in his rain coat.

"Where to buddy?" The hack pushed down the meters.

"The waterfront, Pier Eleven. A ship called the Hiroshi Maru sails in an hour. Can you make it?"

"No sweat. We still got an hour before the morning rush starts."

The taxi splashed through a puddle of rain as it turned the corner.